M000313835

SPANGLED RUIN

Holly Morse

SPANGLED RUIN

TALL ISLAND PRESS
New York, New York
2017

Published by Tall Island Press
New York, New York

Spangled Ruin is a work of fiction. All names, characters, places, and incidents
either are products of the author's imagination or are used fictitiously.

Printed in the United States of America
Design by Andrew Tennant

ISBN 978-0-9913272-9-4

Cover Design by Ashley Siebels

For Asher,
who lit up the world.

Contents

Delivery

Slot. Slot. Slot. Slot. Slot. After all these years, it was still gratifying. May savored the slight force required to slip envelopes into the narrow openings. The sound of dropped mail interrupted her. May shifted her attention to the far end of the mailroom. There was "the hand." She did not immediately turn away from her work. She posted the last letters. May knew everybody in town by name but she sometimes thought of the residents by a feature of their anatomy. Roy Turner, whose rosacea, in combination with steady sun exposure and drink, had made a bulb of his nose, was "the nose." The red headed Ryans were "the gingers." And the owner of a hand curled in on itself was simply "the hand." May shrugged her shoulders and scanned the boxes she'd just finished filling. All these orderly metal alcoves, now full. She sighed with satisfaction. "Pigeonholed" came to mind.

Navigating the packages and her desk chair, May moved as best she could in the cramped space, to see what "the hand" needed at the counter. From a few feet away, May saw Eleanor (that was her name) wearing a pale blue sweater. It was an ordinary crew neck but made from some cloud-like yarn. Even up close, the pullover appeared in soft focus. May's own brown cardigan had nubs. A sturdy relative of unparalleled productivity and civic-mindedness had knit it for her.

Before May reached Eleanor, August Walsh bounded into the room and tapped Eleanor on the shoulder. Eleanor swung around to him. Her medium brown hair had been pulled into a ponytail that hung, like the fringe across her forehead, in a straight fall. The slightest breeze could lift it—May knew because the post office counter was just steps from the front door and she had seen this happen on balmy days—but her hair would drop back into perfect alignment. As Eleanor turned toward August, the ponytail swung wide and settled with the precision of a gymnast's dismount. May wondered if this was its nature or achieved by art. May narrowed her eyes at Eleanor's white slacks. It's money, she thought.

"Hey you," said August. The two looked at each other goofily. August realized he should probably have something to say so he said, "Did you hear about what happened out by Tarpitt Road?"

"Uh-uh."

"Well, it seems a limb was down across the road right by the Maynards' drive. As the crew was clearing it, Buck Maynard accosted our Highway Superintendent."

"Not Joe?" Eleanor sucked in air.

"Joe. Buck was worked up about another limb still on the tree. He insisted it was an even bigger hazard than the one lying across the road. Said the Town had to clear it away."

"Yeah?"

"Yeah. But Joe didn't appreciate being told his job. He said the Highway Department was not responsible for clearing away every last dead limb in town. There was a scene."

"What kind of scene?" asked Eleanor in a hushed voice. May thought Eleanor sounded breathy.

"Buck and Joe got into an argument and it ended with Buck pushing Joe and grabbing his saw. Before anyone could stop him, Buck jumped up on the stone wall by the tree. It seems he was swinging that saw around and no one dared approach. He scrambled up the tree in question, grunting with the weight of the saw, while the whole highway crew tried to shout him down."

"No."

"Yes."

"Isn't Buck Maynard, like, mid-fifties?"

August nodded, "Something like that but, apparently, he used to do tree work. Anyway, Buck got himself up the tree—it was an old spreading beech—and dropped the dead branch easily enough but lost his footing right after and fell along with the branch." Eleanor's good hand flew to her mouth.

"Is he all right?"

"Compound fracture and a concussion."

"Good god."

"Yeah. When the First Responders got there, Joe was still hopping mad. With the bone sticking right out of Buck's shin, Joe began cursing Buck as he came to. Shouting at him it was his own damn fault while they were loading Buck into the ambulance."

"Who told you all this?" asked Eleanor starting to chuckle in spite of herself. The chuckle infected August who tried hard not to, but started laughing freely.

"I heard it from Stoney who heard it from Tom Haight," he snorted. Eleanor was shaking her head.

"It must be true, then."

"Who says nothing ever happens around here?" continued August as he moved past her to open his box. May did not care for the way he said this, rolling in a suggestion of being familiar with much bigger places.

"Whoo," said Eleanor. "I mean, I'm sorry Buck got hurt but . . ." Her shoulders were still jiggling. Now, August was shaking his head. He touched her on the arm as he slid past with his mail.

"Hey, see you at Marianne's on Saturday?"

"You bet."

"OK. Great." August Walsh stood by the door with the light shining around him and smiled back at Eleanor. Although he was just four feet away, she waved at him. When she turned back to the counter, May saw him admire her before leaving. OK, thought May. She liked that Eleanor's hand didn't slow him down.

"Hi," said Eleanor. May looked up at Eleanor's symmetrical face. She considered the young woman on the other side of the counter.

"What can I do for you?"

"Um," said Eleanor, who was struggling to hold her mail in her good hand, having scooped it up from the counter where she'd fumbled it, "I have a slip here for a package." She doesn't know that Buck's dad was a vicious alcoholic, May thought. That he beat his kids and once, during the bad storm of '74, he threw Buck out in the snow. Buck was eight. Lost the top of two fingers from the frostbite. Just plain luck it wasn't worse. Neither of them realize Buck no longer does tree work because Joe's brother opened a larger operation that stole Buck's clients. What Joe knows about clearing limbs he knows from the man who ruined Buck's business. Also, neither of them have any idea that Tom Haight can't tell a straight story to save himself. Tom hasn't been able to tell the truth since fifth grade when he told Mrs. White he didn't make Josie Delgatto drink that jar of pond water. The one they had on the shelf in the science room with tadpole eggs.

May had already heard all this news. But she had heard it right.

May waited while Eleanor put the mail down again on the counter, held it with pressure from the side of her curled hand, and slipped the piece of yellow paper out from under the rubber band that held the bundle together. Although the process was slow, Eleanor did not seem self-conscious. She passed May the slip. May grazed one of Eleanor's long fingers as it released its hold. May wondered about asking but decided to wait. She turned from Eleanor and made her way back to the stack of packages. She retrieved a soft silver pouch from a fancy retailer, some other article of useless clothing perhaps, and returned to the window.

"Here you go," said May and handed it over.

"Thanks," said Eleanor but her eyebrows contracted. She had picked up her mail again, leaving her good hand occupied. She would have to let go of her mail to collect the pouch. May watched Eleanor make a recalculation. She pinned the bundle of letters under her left arm to extend her capable hand to receive the package.

May felt the urge to speak again, to finally say something, and suppressed it a second time. I have been handling her mail for five years, reasoned May. She looked at Eleanor who was on the point of turning to go. May could tell the bundle clamped against the blue sweater was going to slip. The quality of the yarn offered no protection from gravity. No protection from anything really. May reflected on the dropped mail that had drawn her attention to "the hand" in the first place. In her mind, May saw Eleanor's slipped bundle hitting the floor and discharging letters. All these years, May routinely rubber-banded Eleanor's mail before putting it in her box. Eleanor didn't recognize this as special treatment. May did it because she could too easily imagine Eleanor stooping and trying to gather loose pieces after such a spill. She understood the small humiliation this would entail.

"Give that back," ordered May. She reached across the counter and, without further exchange, took back the silver package from Eleanor's strong hand. "Hand me your letters," May directed. Eleanor forked over the bundled mail from under her arm. Quickly, aware of her own dexterity, May lifted the rubber band and, folding the silver pouch in half, slipped it under the band, and handed the larger bundle back. With a little rearranging, Eleanor could manage this by holding everything under her left arm, supported by her strong hand.

"Thank you," Eleanor said. May looked again at the face so at odds with injury.

"I've never asked about your hand," said May, "What happened to it?"

Eleanor, surprised, trained her amber eyes on May. There was weariness, shame, and something else in them. Something hard.

"It's a long story," Eleanor said, "an accident when I was fourteen."

"Oh," said May, "You've had it a long time, then. Must be a nuisance." Eleanor looked at May as if she saw her.

"It is. Thank you for asking." There was a pause. Eleanor tossed her head, swinging her ponytail to one side. "You can't imagine how often people don't even notice."

"Oh, I can," said May. An inquiring look crossed Eleanor's face. May was reminded of a doe in a field at a human's approach, curious and not yet ready to flee. Now, thought May. Out of sight, behind the counter, May lifted her heavy foot and felt its awkward weight.

Goats

Yes, my abiding passion was to start-up a farm and make cheese somewhere amazeballs. Instead, for the last four years, I'd been doing night work, as a proofreader for a law firm midtown. I'd been at this awhile, holed up on a questionable corner in Clinton Hill. It sucked—the part about misusing my degree for this bottom-feeder task. Also, rarely seeing daylight. Still, with the combo, I'd saved sort of a third of what was needed for a down payment on a small chunk of rural life. At the time, I thought it was friggin' outlandish how little things cost if they're in average shape away from the bullseye of town. And, when the dream was hatched, I had a pretty reasonable boyfriend who was good at pretty much everything. He was especially good at patinas—on plaster, on wood, on concrete. He'd gone to RISD. He wears a mun.

Since we're talking hair, I should clarify, I'm not Heidi or anything just because I have an interest in herds and, as it turns out, hoary old men. My hair is jet black for shit sake. Not dye either. Black like a pirate's heart. I would tell you I went to Oberlin but I know where you're gonna go with that. Forget it. Anyway, I'm digressing.

Suddenly, something happens.

I travel to the country on an eye-searing day. Blue everywhere and the beeches screaming yellow. It's October and my uncles have loaned me their house for the weekend. I'm not done with the boyfriend but he is unaccountably sort of done with me. I would be grieving like Margaret, you know, "over golden groves unleafing," except the fates have arranged a different grief. My father, who I'd never particularly known, died. It turned out that while he was busy ignoring us, he'd been out West making a bundle. The app was clever enough but not so clever that if it came to you, you'd, like, hit yourself on the forehead and shout "eureka!" or anything. It was a case of the right place at the right time.

Even so, his death launched me. Or the whole trifecta did. I had a vacancy sign over my vag, the foliage had turned, and so had my fortunes. It seemed there was no deep reason to stall. Happiness would find me, I thought blithely.

I'm in this altered state, buoyed by my sunny nature, when I turn off the Taconic. I'm about 30 minutes from my uncles' place and 15 minutes from the first farm. I pass through a village with a farm-store, so sweet it made my eyes sting. Even just from the outside. Something about the wash on the stucco and the bushels of apples in a friggin' spectrum of red pushed up against the wall. I would get some livestock and soon my chevre would be displayed in there. With grey labels and the inevitable too-thin hipster font, styled like it was spastically hand-drawn. Patinaed with quiet sophistication.

Then, of course, I think of the boyfriend.

So when my GPS tells me to head down a dirt road and turn in, on the left, through a cow-gate, the blush is off the rose. The farm is deserted. I look in the cracked windows of the farmhouse while I wait. Impossible to say, without making entry, what could be salvaged. I'm about to head out back to check out the barn when a car pulls in. Then another, a black Audi.

Great, I think, the realtor has made an appointment to show the property simultaneously to me and some wealthy douchebag. The real estate agent is all over herself apologizing but there is nothing for it. Crossed lines of communication she says.

The guy is about six four and old. Not over-the-hill old but the kind of got-your-shit-together old where your skin suggests world-class product. Maybe the ghost of the beginning of jowls. When does that happen? Everything about him is interestingly smooth—his jeans, his voice, his leather boots. He greets me like it pains him to have interrupted my private showing. I mean, like it really pains him but he doesn't give a fuck either. I couldn't guess his age. Forties maybe?

"Max Eld," he says, shooting out his hand. Of course you are, I think. His hand is agreeably dry.

"Vivienne," I say. I'd be damned if I was going to give this Viking my real name.

"So sorry to have intruded. If it is a terrible trouble I can reschedule." He pronounces the H in schedule and not the C. Not sure if this is legit. I mumble something non-committal. The sun is in his eyes. They are super blue.

"Shall we start with the house?" says the realtor.

"If you don't mind, I'd rather start with the barn," says the Viking.

"Fine by me," I say.

We trudge out across the pasture while Max tells me he is looking at several "locations." I wonder, for what, but don't ask. Then he gives a mad swat at something near his eye and does a stumbling sidestep into me. He almost knocks me over.

He says "shit" instead of "sorry." I'm amused until, in that same split second, he grabs my arm and continues the awkward two-step, hauling me along until we're both relocated and parked near an old truck. Light glancing off its side mirror is reflected across his big face with its swelling brow. Then, I look back and see bees, pissed off, hovering low to the ground. He is squinting sort of in the same direction. I catch the agent nervously skirting the nest on the other side. She looks all elbows, the white of her inner arms exposed. Max makes a sound. I turn, smiling. In a flash of horror, I realize, he is gasping for air.

He wheezes, "Epipen in my car . . . glove compartment." I turn but he grabs my arm again so hard he is bruising me. With his other hand, he's reaching, in desperation, for the front of his pants. I'm confused-while-scared until it comes to me. The keys. The car is locked. I bat his hand away and plunge mine into his pocket. I feel them in there, hard and reassuring. I yank them out and run.

Later, in the ambulance, the tip of his nose is still unnaturally white and he is shaking from the epinephrine in the shot. He can't say much but he can breathe. I find I'm telling him about the five major dairy goats in America. That Alpine can produce up to two gallons a day. About butterfat and quantity. How most farmers mix their stock. I reveal I love LaMancha and Nubian breeds best. With his drug-induced tremors, he nods.

"What if we had made the barn?" I ask. "We would have stepped inside. It would be vast in there." I pause. "Post and beam," I say, "hay-covered floor."

Backbone

Flexibility, strength, and endurance. These were the words Martin heard as the physiotherapist swung past the wall with purple heating pads hung over pegs. Jeff liked to scoot around the room on his rotating stool. Martin supposed it made the therapist feel like his time was important. Martin thought the heating pads looked like saddles for an army of miniature ponies.

While continuing his pep talk, Jeff retrieved a skeleton shoulder from a shelf of models. Martin already knew swinging his arm overhead had inflamed his shoulder and that made his subsomething space smaller. The tight socket had squashed things, over and over, when he played ball. A surgeon had fixed the tear. Now, Jeff was helping Martin get his swing back.

Martin imagined grinding the toes of his baseball cleats into the sand on the pitcher's mound. More than anything he wanted to be there on that mound. He was an All Stars pitcher for his Major Division team. He was even willing to humor Jeff, who'd returned with his fake bones. At least Martin thought they were fake. Do they let everyone who needs them just have real skeleton parts? Are there extra skeletons lying around somewhere? Martin imagined a pile of bones in the closet where they keep the Little League bats and catchers' chest protectors.

"Well, kiddo, this is how it works," began Jeff. Martin was not tall for twelve. Knucklehead Moloney was already shooting up as Martin's mom said. She was the one who first called him "knucklehead." Not because he was white either. It started when she caught Moloney trying to get a group of them to put lighter fluid in a super-soaker to make a flamethrower. Martin bet it would have worked. She said Knucklehead Moloney's growth spurt was early and not to worry. Martin wasn't worried. He wasn't tall but he wasn't too short either.

Jeff was knocking the bones around in front of Martin. He draped the skeletal arm over his shoulder to show Martin the socket up close. Martin giggled. It looked like Jeff was dancing with it.

"Listen, I'm not sure what's so funny but I want you to pay attention. OK?"

Martin nodded.

"It looks a little like you're dancing with the skeleton."

"Oh, I see," said Jeff, taking the arm off his shoulder. He settled himself more squarely on his stool and got serious with Martin about the joint. Martin made every effort to get serious too. He even repeated "sub-acromial." Jeff lit up after that. The pores on his nose looked big when he smiled.

Martin was happy to leave the office. He liked Jeff but, seriously, why did he need so much information? Just the exercises and the reps please.

Normally, Martin would hop on his bike to get around town. But since he could not ride with his arm like this, his mom was letting him walk the short distance to school. She would drop him off before work and, with warnings not to dawdle and to be careful crossing the streets, she trusted him to make his way safely to school, on foot, until he was better. It wasn't so bad. It meant he missed second period on Mondays. To get to school there was the plaza with the P.T. clinic, an empty stretch of road with weedy scrub, the railroad track, Pond Road with Black Pond, and then Riverton Middle School.

It was along the empty bit right before the railroad tracks that the red car slowed and kept pace with Martin. They rolled down the passenger window.

"Hey blimpy, want a ride?"

Martin glanced over. There were two teenagers in the car. He'd seen one of them around before. The car was faded to pink across the hood. A bumper was coming loose from the body. Martin turned his attention to the ground and kept walking. He could think of things to shoot back but knew better. He wasn't fat. It was all muscle.

"You looking for wontons?" called the other guy. The first teen thought this remark extremely entertaining. Martin heard them both cracking up. They rolled up their window and pulled ahead but continued slowly. Martin considered his options. He could turn around and sprint back toward the clinic. It would take them time to turn around and, maybe, they wouldn't even bother. Or he could keep walking. If they tried to mess with him, he would take off toward school. He was a pretty fast runner. He hesitated for a moment, thinking. The slurs surprised him. There were only three Chinese families in town: Martin and his mom, the Lees and the Changs. They weren't a group that drew attention.

The car pulled past the tracks. Martin kept walking forward, looking studiously at the ground. When he next looked up, he was only ten feet from the car. It was stopped at the side of the road. The taller kid had gotten out. A shock ran up Martin's short frame.

"It's stalled. Can you help give us a push?" said the teen, his voice weirdly bland. Martin regretted not turning around. The plan to take off toward school would mean passing them before breaking into a run. Martin's heart began to beat faster. He decided to act as if they hadn't heckled him. At least, until they were abreast—put the guy at ease. Martin wished Jeff were there with his stool. Despite his hurt shoulder, he imagined fending these jerks off with the stool like a lion tamer. Jeff would cheer him on.

"Sure," he said and ambled up to the car. It was hard to amble with the blood pulsing in his ears. A slow nasty look spread across the tall kid's face. He was the boy Martin recognized. Once Martin was right at the car, he smelled something sour coming off the kid. Martin wrinkled his nose and moved into position behind the car. He was careful to stand to the right edge of the back bumper. That way he could make a clean get away when the tall boy bent to the left side of the bumper. Instead, the tall boy came up and stood beside him.

"Move over to the other side," he said.

"Can't."

"Why not?"

"Bum shoulder—much better purchase on this side," said Martin.

The tall boy leered down at Martin.

"'Purchase,'" he repeated, imitating a nerd voice. He didn't move but continued to stand not two feet away, between Martin and his easiest point of escape. As Martin was trying to figure out his next best move, the driver appeared, standing on the other side of the car.

"Whaz goin' on here?" he slurred. Maybe that sour smell was alcohol. Martin felt a prickle of sweat break out on his palms. It was only ten in the morning. They both moved in toward Martin. Since the car had clearly not stalled, the whole ruse was aimed to box him in—to get him between them.

"He's got a hurt shoulder," drawled the tall one.

"Aw, that's a shame," said the second teen.

Martin knew then he'd given them exactly the wrong information. He could hear the pop of his shoulder being dislocated or broken. Because of Jeff, he could picture his own bones, the ones that were supposed to glide, and the muscles, and the tendons. He imagined the teens' boozy breath closing over him, the satisfaction of inflicting pain making their eyes shine. Later, the cops would find his mangled body at the bottom of Black Pond.

The taller boy stepped close to Martin and flicked his middle finger hard against Martin's shoulder.

"Is this the one?" he asked, feigning concern. Martin took a deep breath and stepped back. At the same time, the other boy drew a pocketknife from his hip pocket and let it hang by his side. Martin forced himself not to look. Instead, he smiled at them.

"I know where we can get an army of miniature ponies," he said. The big boys froze.

"Whaa?" the tall one began.

"I'm a stable hand, you know, on Monday mornings." Martin spoke slowly and as evenly as he could. The older boys looked at each other too surprised to grasp what was happening. Martin stepped back again, just one step, nothing large or showy, and continued.

"The cool thing is, we could let them out without being caught. Stampede 'em through town." He paused and looked at his would be assailants. "They're worth a fortune." Martin leveled a fierce look into the driver's eyes. "A very rare breed."

"The kid's nuts," the taller one muttered. But before the driver could respond, Martin took another step back and was speaking again.

"It's right back the way I came," Martin paused and connected again with the driver's eyes.

"Are you in?" Martin pronounced this last question so gamely the two teens could not contain themselves. Their laughter was the break Martin needed. As they erupted in guffaws, Martin turned and sprinted off, counting the distance under his breath, "Three feet, six, nine." When he thought he was at forty-six feet, his pitching distance, he spun around, spying, and scooping up a rock as he turned. It was a graceful all-in-one movement, the movement of an athlete. The teenagers had barely moved. They were still gripping each other laughing, struck helpless by the ponies. Overtaking this hefty Asian kid would be a breeze.

Martin aimed right for the tall boy's head, recruiting every ounce of his training. In a searing arc, he wound up and pitched the rock hard and true. It struck the big kid above his ear. The sharp edge of the stone cut through the boy's hair and scalp. Martin saw blood leaking across the thug's ear. Now, the driver sprung forward.

"You little shit," he yelled. But before he'd covered half the distance, a second stone connected with this boy's nose with an audible *CLOCK*. The howl the large boy let out was rage and pain in equal measure. Holding his now-limp arm, Martin ran for the clinic. His breath pressed his ribs out against the barrel of his chest, again and again, but his speed remained steady. By the time the plaza was within easy reach, Martin was more aware of the sensation in his shoulder than the effort the run was costing him in other ways. He risked looking back. The big boys and their car were gone. Martin stopped. He recalled the look he'd exchanged with the driver right before he'd made his break—the teens' eyes unfocused and too old for his face as if he'd already witnessed, and was mourning, a world of wars with unthinkable casualties. Martin slowed to a walk, continuing to prop up his arm, light headed. He was eager to pass his suffering off to Jeff. Before he fainted, six yards from the clinic door, Martin spun around, once, like a wooden top. Just as his eyes closed, he saw a cloud in the shape of a stallion.

Blue Mountain

In Minnesota, Katja opened her eyes. Overhead the perforated tiles of the ceiling were all she could see. She remembered her dream. I am aware that I can fly and I boast about it to a crowd of onlookers. The feeling is familiar. As soon as I sense my hidden ability, I rise up on my toes and then continue to rise until I am off the ground. Keeping in constant touch with knowing I can fly is what makes it possible. I am now up above the room. I swoop through, very sure of myself, and therefore able to direct my movements. I brush by and kiss a man who is enamored by my powers. Behind him, a girl in a dark doorway wears a crown. She gives off light.

Thirty-five minutes later, Jon took the stairs. Already in bed, Lucia had just put her glasses and book on the bedside table. Without them, he looked blurry in the doorway. She snapped off the light. Earlier, a display of flowers had blown into her brain as she worried a hangnail—flowers just picked from a garden: red ones, and white, and some, like the famous *Semper Augustus*, "broken" in streaks of red and cream. She wanted a large overfull vase nearby, perhaps on a side table. What she had in mind would have required a garden. Not just a tidy border either, with a spring show of bulbs, but a formal garden, the kind kept by staff, with beds devoted to tulips, grouped by color, bounded by boxwoods, so that dozens and dozens could be cut for the great room without making a dent. And there would have to be a great room, with paned doors overlooking the beds. The house, its gardens, and great room were just a backstory. What captured Lucia's imagination was the wanton spill of wealth—blooms overarching each other, open, trailing their era, their viral variegation, their viscera: gluey pistils, dusty stamen. The arrangement's spectral presence visited again, briefly, in the corner of the bedroom. It was this ghost, and the scent on her fingers from touching herself, that would draw Jon to her.

"Sorry it took me so long, Lu," said Jon, exhausted, as he crawled in beside her. Instantly, he noticed the space alive between them. The charge intensified as if coming from her. It proved stronger than his lethargy. Jon rolled toward Lucia. "Hey," he said. With this consent, she extended her long fingers, lacing them through his hand. Jon grasped and pulled her close, a vision of wet, yielding flags sluicing through him. Enlarged, like the sticky knob on a plant, and growing, he bloomed in the darkness. Jon Dover made a guttural sound.

Katja, in the everlasting blue night, blinked.

Weak morning light leaked through the blind's slats, streaking the lab table. In his white coat, Jon lunged forward onto one knee—the pull along his hamstring a pleasant counterpoint to the data in front of him. He stood upright and clicked through the page. He stopped stretching and began practiced small hops, his toes barely leaving the floor of the laboratory. Jon usually ran to work, 3 ½ miles, five days a week, when the weather was warm, unless demands cut short his time. Jon opened his arms wide and then wrapped them across his chest. The study was close to completion. He just needed the results on the last trial to factor in. Even in neuroscience, no single set of keys could unlock the secret of personality disorders. He stopped hopping. He thought about depression and co-morbid addiction in borderlines. Why were these conditions so often linked? Concentrated, Jon disappeared into his topic. The sun momentarily warmed his ankle but he barely noticed.

In the treatment group for the phototherapy study, patient 117 had responded particularly well to the light box. He wondered if number 117 was Susanna, a sex addict. He wondered if this affliction was what had brought her to mind.

Susanna limped, the consequence of a fractured hip in childhood. When he took her history, Jon thought the evidence pointed toward her father. Susanna bore the standard psychological scars of abuse: her compulsion to repeat dangerous sex, her complicated relations with men, a failed marriage, gaps in memory. She also had attempted suicide. One attempt preceded the study by only eighteen months. Jon hadn't wanted to use her for this reason but had been won over by his colleague, Tere Fernandez, because Susanna had been in DBT (dialectical behavioral therapy) longer than others in the study. During her intake, Jon noted her classic borderline presentation, the play of flirtatiousness and deep suspicion in her eyes. Given the nature of the disorder, there was going to be suicidality. One had to resign oneself to that.

Jon looked at the spike in the data and was curious.

Across campus at the museum, Lucia scrolled through a preselection of work from the art collaborative, HIRA. Her assistant was finalizing shipment from Japan. Lucia squinted at wave patterns woven into cloth. In raking light, the beauty of the cloths' photographic sources jumped out—a breathtaking variety of undulating forms. For this exhibition, the dynamic Japanese team had also produced translucent tubes with etchings at their core. These they scattered on the floor. Shifting light projected toward them caused their inner grooves to appear animated, as if flowing with a mysterious fluid. It was a lot of lighting to get right. Lucia adjusted her pencil skirt. She smiled, fingering the fabric and her professional clout. She imagined a critic writing, "Once again the young curator, Lucia Erikson, champions spectacle."

Katja slept and woke in brief cycles. Is it because the fabric of time is thinning that I know emotions can arrive in the future? Time spills into itself and casts itself forward like salmon upstream, to spawn. This fact is gaining weight as my body disappears.

Jon left the lab as soon as he reasonably could, knowing the world would come back into over-saturated color when he reached home. Cracking the door, he wasn't disappointed. The aroma of veal stew hit him. He felt its painful draw on his saliva glands. He looked through to the kitchen. Everything seemed ticked up a notch.

"It's going to be a spectacular show," called Lucia.

"I'll bet," said Jon. And then, forcing himself to wait a civilizing beat, "What kind of stew?"

Lucia narrowed her eyes as she stirred the pot. It had been a little over twelve months, right before the last winter break, since she watched the precise way Jon filled his plate at the cafeteria. She had been fascinated by how he portioned out the meatballs and their sauce. Jon broadcast lab-rat, but despite this, because he was lanky and handsome and had extraordinary hands, she had inched her tray closer and said, "I'm Swedish too. Like those balls you're organizing."

He had looked back surprised but laughed. He saw right away she was too cool for him. Luckily, her dazzling surface had sharpened his clinical instincts, so he also detected a raw center. Then the observation was lost the next moment when, as innocently as a clam, he had opened himself to those freakish pale eyes.

Lucia moved in with Jon two months later.

As she came to know him, his portioning made Lucia wonder if it was an effort to camouflage, rather than control, how much food he needed to consume. At times, she thought him like an animal over its kill—careful and possessive. Once, when she was in the middle of her period, she looked at his plate and found herself put off. His sorting showed type, she thought.

Often, however, because she was infatuated, this tick was beguiling. She was used to eccentrics. The art world was chock-a-block with them. For instance, she knew a dealer in Berlin whose apartment was littered with loose change because he couldn't pick coins up off the floor—had a phobia or something. From a certain angle, the patterns Jon made with his food appeared like a code she couldn't read, communication from an alien tribe. She pictured his impressive brain driving an urge for measured provisions—a powerful instrument needing precise fuel.

Tonight was like that. Lucia sat enjoying him while Jon marshaled, then demolished, half the stew. She watched him clear up. "I was thinking, Jon, about having a cocktail party the Friday after next."

"Why?"

"I want to throw a pre-show reception—just a few couples, that hideous new chief curator, and the artists arriving for the opening."

"But isn't next Friday the 13th?"

"So?"

"I don't know—bad luck?"

"Jon, don't be insane." She looked fondly at his back bent over the sink. "It's *Jul* on the 13th."

"*Jul?*"

"How can you not know this? Sweden's Saint Lucia's Day. In the morning there are saffron buns and candles. At night, we drink *glögg*."

"Your day?'

"Yes."

"What were we doing last year?"

"Fucking, I think."

Jon turned from his chore and looked at Lucia sitting at the table, her small feet propped on the bottom rung of his chair, her bleached bangs electrifying her face. Lucia adjusted her glasses.

"Oh, yeah." Jon stepped from the sink and moved to her with a mad lurch. He stood looking down at her as if she were Frankenstein's bride. Lucia laughed. He ran a sudsy, gloved hand behind her neck. With his other hand he pulled the neck of her sweater aside and kissed the scar that marked her shoulder. One day he would get to the bottom of its mystery.

"Eew, get off me." Lucia snorted as she pushed at his chest.

"She's alive!' he croaked as he bent toward her laughing face. At the last moment, when he was inches away, he dropped the act. Lucia tipped her head back against the wet glove, her mouth wide from laughing, and kissed him.

Susanna stood awkwardly by the front door of her apartment. There was a dim hall mirror above the radiator on her right. She counted the keys on her key ring. She counted them one by one to six, repeated the ritual and then repeated it again. Susanna looked up at the mirror. The hair above her eyes made a soft sweep, a 1940's wave of gold. The gods allowed her to be flooded with toxic ungovernable feelings but had bestowed this gift, a glamorous note that made her look, as one drunk said, like a dame in a detective story.

Irrational urges were overtaking her. She could not meet her own gaze. That feeling, like scurrying insects, raced up her inner thighs. She felt the promise of the coming sting and bite. She let herself linger in anticipation as the swarm spread. She shook her keys, furtively caught her reflection, and opened the door.

Jon scanned notes on his tablet while Lucia read, hunkered down among the pillows. She flinched when Jon's phone buzzed on the side table.

"It's Fernandez," said Jon.

"Don't answer it. It's almost eleven thirty."

"No, I'd better . . ." He sighed as he reached for the phone. "Hello, Tere?" He listened and sat up straight.

"What is it?" whispered Lucia.

"Yeah, yeah. Where?" Jon paused. He continued to listen for a long stretch. "Jesus." Lucia tugged on his arm. Jon held up a finger for her to wait.

"OK. Right." Jon listened. "We can figure that out tomorrow. Yeah, that's likely. OK. No, I don't think so." Jon bent his head and closed his eyes. He exhaled through his nose. Gently he said, "I hope so, Tere. OK. Thanks for the heads-up." Jon put down the phone and stared straight ahead.

"What is it?" asked Lucia again.

"Cops found the wallet of a patient in the study."

"So?"

"It had blood on it." He shook his head slightly. They exchanged a meaningful look. Lucia knew he was working with borderlines. Jon's features fell into a professional frown.

"How'd they reach you?"

"It had Fernandez's card in it."

She clicked her tongue sympathetically. "How do you manage to work with this population?"

Jon put his head in his hands. "Fernandez sent one of the research assistants. If he can find the patient, and she's all right, he can get her to services and bypass the police until she's sober." Jon was struggling not to experience his fear that this event, depending on what it was exactly, could scuttle his project.

"Why?"

Jon shot her *the look*—like a spook with sensitive intel. Lucia knew its meaning. She knew better than to ask for patient details he was not allowed to share.

"But the cops are looking too?" she asked.

"Of course."

At midnight, the call came in.

On a guess, the assistant circled closer to Susanna's apartment by a back route. Coming around a corner, he saw one white leg, missing its shoe, sticking out from under a bush. As the assistant approached, he felt his chest tighten. In medical school, he'd cut into cadavers like everyone else. But if she were dismembered . . .

> *As a girl, Katja collected pebbles at the seaside. She would look for ones with rings around them, for luck. Dark smooth stones with white bands were her favorites. She hoarded them in her room, showing them off to her little cousins. She adored the salt air. She remembered lying on her stomach on the rocks, looking into the bay where the water was very clear and watching the zostera marina trailing its leaves up, sometimes a meter long, from the sandy bottom. Growing up was the business of finding each new device—ringed rock, shooting star, four-leaf clover, plucked petals.* These discoveries, like stepping-stones, would take you on your lucky way.

As the assistant crossed to the hedge, there was time for him to consider why he'd chosen psychiatry over primary medicine. Steeling himself, he lifted the branches out of the way. Susanna lay in a heap, the other leg splayed at a weird angle. Blood leaked from her nose. Before stooping to find a pulse, he searched for evidence of breathing. She stirred, opened a swollen eye, and began to ramble. Eventually he understood; she was insisting it was just her limp that had made her fall.

Jon called the precinct. He explained about her different medications. The cops, once they knew she was mentally ill and under care, lost interest in the full story. Jon spoke with the on-call psychiatrist and arranged to have Susanna kept overnight at the local hospital. Jon would check in and provide his impressions in the morning.

Waiting for this business to finish, Lucia became irritable. It was one in the morning. To make up for the drama, Jon spooned behind her to help her drift off. Lucia knew perfectly well Jon could not lie like this without becoming aroused, despite the earlier toss. Ignoring him satisfied an ungenerous itch for payback. Soon she was asleep.

When he arrived in the morning, Susanna was sitting on the bed in a hospital gown. Bruises darkened the side of her face. Her thin mouth erupted in a swollen seam. One hand was bandaged. He thought he'd been prepared, but he was shocked. He looked at her chart to steady himself. It recorded other contusions along her side. What if the outcome had been worse? For a split second he felt like a kid caught tampering with something dangerous. All the patients in the study were receiving DBT. But only those in the treatment group were also getting the light therapy. What if Susanna wasn't one of them? What if she were merely a control and he wasn't providing the best he believed he had to offer? He pulled down on the lapels of his lab coat.

"Hello, Susanna. How are you feeling?"

She spat at him, "Does this mean, I'm out of your study?"

"No, not necessarily." She didn't answer. He moved to the side of her bed and sat on the chair. She shot him a pleading look. He knew all of this—her rapidly shifting moods and manipulativeness—the kaleidoscope of her disease. Jon felt a swell of compassion.

"Do you want to tell me what happened?"

"It was a mistake," she whispered.

"Did a stranger do this to you?"

Susanna shot back a hostile look. "Who said that?"

"No one. I'm just trying to understand." She went mute again and seemed to be struggling.

"You don't care about me. Nobody does. I'm worthless."

"Susanna, you know these harsh judgments aren't true." He paused. When she offered nothing new, Jon used his bedside tone. "I want to know, so I can figure out how to help. Did you seek anonymous sex?" Susanna looked at him as if she might attack him.

"Yes. Yes. Yes."

"A bar?"

"I found a guy and we drank." She leered at Jon. Then, her shoulders slumped. "It got rougher than I meant."

Jon sighed. "That's why it's so important to stick with your program." He cleared his throat and softened his voice, "You can't control how rough the sex gets." Susanna looked wide-eyed, accused, and bewildered. "Here is what I would like to suggest. I would like you to stay over tonight. I've prescribed something to help you rest. When you are feeling better tomorrow, we'll meet for a full session and decide what steps we can take to get you back on track."

Susanna looked away again.

"OK?" He prompted.

"If I miss several days, I can't continue in the study."

"I didn't say that."

Suddenly, Susanna grabbed Jon by the sleeve. Jon jerked back. She raised an eyebrow, mocking his recoil. She let go and Jon adjusted his sleeve, once again collecting himself.

"What did you want to say?"

Susanna's look shifted, her eyes bottomless yet mirroring. "I think the therapy was helping."

"It may well be, Susanna. Why don't you rest now? We will have a regular meeting when you are feeling better." Susanna went absent as a dreamy child. "I'll look in on you, tomorrow." She said nothing more, so Jon turned to go. When he walked out into the hallway, he heard Susanna release her breath as if she had been holding it.

On Friday, December 13th, Jon was stationed at the door, the greeter for the *Jul* fest. Ever awkward at these things, he inadvertently let the neighbor's white cat slink in with the arriving guests. He left his post to try to corral it, but the cat was too fast for him, slipping among the company. As it disappeared around the kitchen counter, Jon gave up the chase and was about to return to the door when Tere tapped him on the shoulder. Jon steered her to the drinks through a room already half full. Lucia's party was off to a rollicking start. Jon and Tere strained to hear as they exchanged information about Suzanna's stabilization. It didn't really matter if Jon could hear Tere. He knew she was pleased they hadn't lost a subject from the final phase.

Quickly, the rooms warmed up. Jon looked to see if Lucia had noticed and saw the cat prowling around her legs. Jon signaled to Lucia the need for air, pantomiming cracking a window. She shook her head, indicating she didn't understand him and couldn't be bothered to figure out what he was play-acting as she was taken up. The difficult new curator had cornered her in conversation. Jon saw her shift impatiently from foot to foot. He thought about rescuing her when the door opened again.

Late enough to ensure an audience, a petite woman in black preceded three young men, fit and exactly matched in size. HIRA had made its entrance. They might be mistaken for a tumbling troupe. The leader wore her hair closely cropped and oiled. She reminded Jon of a seal. Down to their glasses, the entire collaborative was in art gear rebooted through Japanese techno. Oozing awareness of their fame, edgier than acrobats, more cerebral than pop stars, they reeked of condescension. Oh, they could stoop to small talk but they made sure you knew their first charge was to satisfy themselves. They were artists. And not just any artists but the type that worked as a group, traveled internationally, and gained notoriety by pooling resources. Jon was suddenly filled with a vision of their mobile lives. In Jon's mind, their fame was just a backstory. What captured his imagination was the freedom of their work, being able to shape shift with the currents of fashion—able to capture attention and access fluidly. Jon stared at the woman. Was she wearing patent leather? As Lucia broke free, crossing the crowded apartment to shake the hand of one of the collective, Jon went to fix himself another drink.

Jon felt swept up in an unusual mood. Maybe it was the *glögg*. He felt both tipsy and gaining clarity at an accelerating pace. But what was he getting clearer on? He looked across the room of hipsters and admired Lucia's *Julboard*—traditional offerings of pickled herring, red cabbage, beet salad, lox, black bread and cheese. He had the inner sense that, although they were swirling through different parts of the party, his thoughts and Lucia's were aligning. When her friend, Signe, turned up with a variant of the saffron buns, a large braided affair, Jon thought he heard a general cry go up.

He fell into several short conversations but was inevitably interrupted by the duties of host. He and Lucia finally met up in the kitchen.

"It's going great," he assured her. She smiled and kissed him on the ear. Unlike Jon, Lucia was a strong partier. Signe swept in, making large gestures with her plump hands.

"Go out with your guests. They don't need any more food," she urged, "I'm bringing the bread. It's almost midnight." Jon took Lucia's hand and dragged her into the living room. Lucia broke his grip to greet another late arrival.

The head of HIRA, Cleo Tanaka, tapped Jon's sleeve. "You are Lucia's husband?" she asked with only the faintest Japanese accent. Now, looking down at her, her stature struck him. Jon thought what a lot of power was compressed in her frame. Lucia seemed almost rangy by comparison. He examined Cleo's oiled head as she lifted her chin to meet his inspection. Anime-style make-up exaggerated her eyes. Her shiny top was stitched in tight horizontal rows like a breastplate.

"We aren't married but this is our place, yes."

"Partners, then. And are you also in the arts?"

"No, I'm a psychiatrist, a researcher."

"Ah," said Cleo. Immediately, her eyes shifted to survey the room beyond his elbow. "It is a lovely party." Cleo paused. "I believe Lucia said this is a festival night for Swedes?"

"Yes," said Jon, helpless to think of a single thing to add. She held out her hand. Jon took it. Cleo gave him a stiff smile and, nodding into the vacuum of his response, moved on. Jon felt gutted by her obvious boredom. He defended himself by locating Lucia across the room. In her midnight blue sheath she was a totem—an emblem of elegance. And he was interesting enough for her.

At just this moment, Signe entered from the kitchen holding aloft the platter with the braided, glazed bread. It was decorated with a ring of candles. As a woman standing next to her lit the candles, Signe nodded to someone to kill the lights and turn off the music. Softly, Signe began to sing a Swedish seasonal song. For all its folksy innocence, it was perfectly on key. Signe sang a little louder, gaining her voice, as she began to cross the room, cake held high, toward Lucia, framed by the doorway behind her. A few Swedes in the crowd joined in.

Lucia's face, caught in a grin as the lights went down, froze. Signe, absorbed by her performance, continued with a steady gait, her warm voice filling the room. Her gesture, this child's song, was at odds with the sophistication of the crowd. Jon tried to read the faces of the collective. They were non-committal—neither judging nor participating. As he followed Signe's progress, her voice faded for him. In its place was an odd buzzing sound. Jon wondered again if there were something in the punch. He looked toward Lucia and noticed the white cat on the back of the couch by the doorway. The cat looked directly at him. She opened her mouth in a yawn. He could see the pink of her tongue. Now the buzzing was resolving into words. It was as if the cat were speaking. The animal seemed to say, "It is happening again."

Caught up in the dream-like moment, Jon shifted his gaze to the clock that showed it was twelve and back to Lucia's face. The candlelight was reflected in her eyes. She opened her mouth wider as if she were in pain. Signe took a last step toward her friend and stopped short, catching Lucia's expression. The action of Signe's quick stop cast the cake forward. One of the lit candles fell, grazing the hem of Lucia's shift. Lucia let out an unexpected and horrible cry as if she were being burnt alive.

Katja's breathing temporarily quickened. Frozen by her condition, her body was nevertheless moving forward, shifting . . .

I feel like the zostra grass rocking in the sea's embrace.
I've become thin and tall just like the grass. I'm reaching
upwards toward the surface. On the other side, will I find
my child self, lying on my stomach, looking down through
the water?

The candle that had hit Lucia's dress tumbled to the floor and
went out. Jon ran toward Lucia, pushing through the crowd
that surged around her. Jon could hear Signe calming her friend
gently in Swedish.

"Let me through," he said with a doctor's authority. The
party shifted and made an opening. Between their shoulders,
he could see the top of Lucia's head. She was looking down—
her white-blond crown like a winter fox's fur in moonlight.
When he was within a foot, she suddenly looked up, finding
his eyes.

"I am so sorry, everyone," she said. "It is nothing. Please, it's
nothing. Go back to the party!" No one moved. Jon reached his
arms out and gathered her in. She briefly rested her head on his
chest and then pulled back. "For god's sake, somebody put the
music back on!" She shouted with false cheer. A guest obliged
and the well-lubricated crowd oozed back to fill their corners of
the room, leaving the couple with each other. Even Signe,
putting down the saffron cake and blowing out the remaining
candles, lingered only long enough to pat Lucia's hand.

"Are you all right?" asked Jon.

"Yeah, now."

"What was *that?*"

Lucia shrugged. Jon did not press her. He observed the room.

"Well, your guests have recovered."

Lucia looked around at the merry group.

"Yeah. Bastards." Jon chuckled and moved to hug her but Lucia hung back.

"I think I need some water."

"Do you want me to get it for you?"

Lucia cut him a sideways glance. "I'm not a fucking invalid, Jon, just freaked out."

"Lu?" He asked as she began to move away.

"Mm?"

"What does *Jul* celebrate?" Lucia looked at him strangely. "Google it," she said.

Katja cast her mind back. She remembered the days when excitement would build. She spoke with hushed reverence of supernatural events. She thought it wrong to mislead but relished whispering tales into small ears.

Troubled, Jon stumbled toward the kitchen following Lucia. He found her at the sink with her back to the room. Something about her posture seemed different to him.

She turned toward him with the glass of water half raised. The look of pain had returned to her face.

"Are you all right?" he asked again.

"I'm cold."

Jon rolled on his side and opened his eyes. The light through the thin curtain was blinding. His head ached. He reached his hand behind him but there were only the warm rumpled sheets. He listened and could hear the shower go on. Jon took a breath and rolled on his back. He reviewed the events of the party and allowed himself to linger, prostrate and hung over, without any of it coming together. He decided it was all an alcohol-induced miasma of odd impressions. He must have been very drunk. Talking cats. Jon heard the shower go off. When the bathroom door cracked opened, a cloud of steam was released and Lucia stepped into the light—the outline of her body bright.

"What was Signe's song?" he asked.

Lucia looked at him.

"It celebrates Saint Lucia." Her brows furrowed. Without taking her eyes off him, standing very straight, she translated: *In places unreached by sun, the shadows brood. Into our dark house she comes, bearing lighted candles.*

"Come back," he said, patting the bed. Lucia squinted, her soft lips making an even line.

"No," she said, "I'm up."

"Then why are you so naked?" he teased.

"I just am."

On Saturday, the HIRA show opened to a large crowd. All of the lighting worked, the effects stunning. Lucia negotiated the museum gallery, glad-handing the necessary people, visibly delighted by the reception. By pre-arrangement, Jon came late but saw the evening through to its conclusion. These events were not his favorite pastime. Lucia was gracious, steering a cute grad student, with hair whiter than her own, toward him to amuse him.

By the 18th the tension between them was lifting. Still, having dragged his feet, Jon could feel Christmas breathing down his neck. He had not yet gotten Lucia's gift. He toyed with the idea of a piece of jewelry—something important—but realized his chance of a stylistic error was too great.

Trudging back across campus in the dark, with the smell of snow in the air, it came to him. The academic time between

January and March was dreary and yet disappeared quickly. He would take her on a trip for spring. Not Paris or New York. Somewhere meaningful to her. That night, searching destinations, he was excited to discover that the University's spring break coincided with another festival. *Våffeldagen*, the Swedish Feast of the Annunciation. It was both the start of spring and beginning of Easter. It was colorful. Children dressed up as witches to celebrate. He'd hit the jackpot. How lucky. As he was reading up on the holiday, Lucia walked in. Jon clicked the page closed as fast as he could and spun his chair around.

"Porn?"

"Very funny," he said.

"Oh, it's fine with me if . . ."

"What? No. Are you kidding?"

Lucia just wagged her head from side to side. "It's no big deal." She paused then asked, "Listen, do you want to go for a drive?"

"Now?"

"Yeah."

"It's late."

"Well, there's an overlook a student told me about. I'm sort of up for it. We can bring a bottle of wine and a blanket." Jon could not believe his ears. Things were really turning around. He was out of his seat before giving his answer.

"Suit up, I'll get the wine."

"Great. I'll drive," she said.

The view was indeed beautiful with the town's lights starry in the dark landscape. Lucia extended her plastic cup from behind the wheel. The mood in the car started to sparkle too. Jon just wanted to be sure she was ready. He strayed lightly from topic to topic while he moved his hand over her knee. At this delicate juncture, a black car pulled up at a little distance and stopped.

"Oh, shit," he said.

"What? It's ok."

"No, they're too close."

"Too close for what?" asked Lucia playfully.

"I can see in their windows," said Jon. As he said this, he glanced over and was surprised that action was already taking place. The car, barely parked, was steaming up. Jon could definitely make out fumbling. Suddenly, a moon of flesh was pressed boldly against the glass. Lucia dropped her head into her hands, giggling.

"Lu, get the car going. We should move." Lucia was helpless with laughter. Jon looked across. The offending body part had disappeared but he could now see two people through the fogged glass with more exposed flesh churning and arranging itself. A second car pulled in and parked just beyond the first. Suddenly, like an image coming into focus, the couple in the first car resolved into a familiar motion, the woman's head bobbing. The man arched himself high enough above the seat, steadying himself with his hands, so the act could not be missed.

"It's dogging," croaked Lucia hysterically.

"It's what?" asked Jon.

"Dogging. People arrange to have public sex and invite others to watch."

"Is that why we're here?" asked Jon, scandalized. Before Lucia could answer, he looked again and saw a face. The woman sliding her mouth over the man's penis was Susanna, absorbed and heedless. The man had freed one hand to splay it across the back of her head. He was pumping her up and down. A protective rush propelled Jon from his seat. Without thinking, he

jumped out, racing around the back of his car. Jon's foot caught
on a rock. He did not fall but was catapulted forward. Lucia
hurried to lower her window fast enough.

"What are you doing?" she shrieked. "Stop it, Jon."

But it was too late. When his hand hit the handle, he swung
open the stranger's car door with the righteousness of rescue.
The performing pair increased their pace. The woman, with
effort, rolled her eye toward him like a whale observing a small
companion fish approaching its side. Jon's glance landed on the
erection as it appeared and disappeared, a dusky shade. He
noticed the woman's pale lips, stretched thin. He felt penetrated
by the sight. His proximity brought on the stranger's shudder-
ing groan. The man rocked the woman's face toward Jon as he
released her. Her mouth turned up, a knowing half-smile leaking milky slime. It took a moment to process that this person
was not Susanna. A heavy blond but no one he knew. Jon's
stomach lurched. He turned halfway back toward Lucia, whose
white face hovered in the car window across the way, a different
chaste and perfect moon, before he vomited on his shoes.

"It's all right, Jon."

Lucia slung her bag on the kitchen table with more force
than she intended. She took a roll of paper towel from below
the counter. Pulling off a sheet and wetting it at the sink, she
handed it to him. Jon quietly accepted the towel. He knelt on
one knee to reach the other shoe. The two strangers' cars had
pulled away as Jon was pulling himself together. What remained
was a sense of dislocation and the thin splatter across his toes.

Lucia watched Jon rub at his shoe. She was standing above
him—somehow unable to move away. It seemed unlike him to
act so impulsively. Particularly where a patient was concerned.

Although it had not been a patient. Lucia tipped her head to the side, studying Jon. She wouldn't care that Jon thought, however briefly, she'd brought them on purpose for the show. She would not object that he'd sunk to such an idea or that it was a sinking.

Jon looked up and directly into Lucia's pale blue eyes. She brought her head upright and pushed her glasses back. The bands in her irises, only slightly brighter than the overall hue, radiated out in starbursts. At the center, Lucia's pupils, like Delphic caverns, suggested prophecy. With one long arm dangling across his bent knee, and still holding the soiled rag, he took a breath. His brain fogged.

"Will you marry me, Lu?" he said.

Involuntarily, Lucia's right hand came to her throat. For an intake of breath, her eyes widened but he found them unreadable. Then, her face clouded. She glanced at the shoe with what she couldn't help thinking of as some other man's cum, threw her head back, and laughed.

Even now, two months later, Jon wondered how their attachment had survived the night. He had been frozen on one knee as Lucia's laugh had faded into silence. Perhaps fused by this awful event rather than thrown apart, they moved through the evening, entering tacitly into an understanding that nothing could be uttered about what had just happened. In the moment, this was their escape hatch—their way of playing for time. Then, as life resumed, the longer it went without a scene, the more it seemed as if his offer had been an illusion. As if he'd never asked at all.

They continued their daily lives. They slept together. They made plans for the immediate future. Despite his own culpability in acting so rashly, something accounted for her rejection beyond the absurdity of the timing. It came from a deep turbulence, maybe even the same place as her terror the night of the *Jul* party. He thought about her scar. He would connect the dots. It was what he was trained to do. Jon would go after her past by stealth. He would discover fragments so slowly she wouldn't resist until he had enough to glue back together the seams of whatever had been broken.

On Christmas Eve, when he handed her the gift in a small box, she untied the satin ribbon slowly, rolling it into a tidy ball. This stalling tipped him off. With his usual clumsiness, he had only thought to delay the revelation. He hadn't anticipated the size of the box might trigger fear of revisiting the marriage proposal.

"It's not what you think," he blurted out.

Lucia lifted her chin. "What do you think I imagine?"

"Never mind," he dodged as, clearly surprised, she drew a Swedish straw goat from its cotton bed. She looked at him bewitched. She picked off some stray cotton. He indicated a bundle on its back tied with red string. Lucia untied it, more briskly this time, and unfolded the square of paper. She flattened the sheet printed with flight information. Laying it in her lap, she glanced up—her pale eyes grateful. She hadn't been to Sweden since she was a child.

The dark months passed. The HIRA show came down. Lucia settled into the rhythm of the scheduling for fall.

When the results of the light-box study were published, they didn't make as big a splash as Jon had hoped, probably because of the small sample size. He rationalized that scientific progress is arduous—trench warfare with small gains and setbacks before sudden sweeping advances. Jon referred Suzanna on to a friend he trusted for her continued care and began designing the next study.

The stroke that had been a last blow to Katja's frame was claiming her now. So little was left. With tremendous effort she broadcast her intention, hoping for its time travel. I am sending love. I am sending love, my darlings, which will reach you in some future.

Their suitcases were ready at the foot of the bed when the letter arrived. Jon was home first and discovered a business envelope addressed to Lucia with the return address of a clinic that offered elder care. He might have put it in the pile of junk mail if it hadn't been addressed by hand and if the facility were not in Minnesota. He had reason now to believe Lucia had lived in Minnesota with her mother and a sister, both of whom she'd lost track of after news of her father's death. Jon had learned she spoke little English when she arrived in America, complicating her early school years. He was certain there had been a trauma: not only because she had no contact with her family, but because he felt it seeping through her skin, in the dark, each time he pried another small detail from her about her past.

It was his turn to cook. He made a simple pasta. Although they were leaving for the airport after dinner, he opened a bottle of wine.

Katja's breathing had developed the audible sign of death's approach. With each breath there was a wet after-gurgle. To the aide checking in, she appeared to have slipped into a final coma. There was no sign of consciousness. A nurse passed in the hallway.

"Is there someone we should be calling?" the aide asked.

"No. We have tried but we have no one on file."

"It's such a shame. Shall I stay with her?" the young woman wanted to know. The nurse stepped in through the doorway. She listened to the rattle.

"Would you? I think that would be a kindness." The young aide nodded solemnly. It would be a first time for her to be with the dying. The nurse nodded back and returned to her rounds. The aide approached the bed. She had heard that, for this kind of lingering demise, you die by stages, starting with the extremities. Tentatively, she touched Katja's feet. Sure enough, they were like ice.

At work, Lucia was trapped in a long programming meeting. She shifted her pen back and forth between her fingers. If they didn't break the meeting up soon, she would have to excuse herself. Despite a fear of planes, she could hardly wait to be airborne. Again, she thought of a garden. They needed to aerate their relationship. Already it was leaching the conditions for fertile feeling. The interest would drain away—everything, even his eating habits, would become tedious and boring.

The aide drew up a chair and was now sitting by Katja, holding her hand. Her breathing was becoming more labored but otherwise Katja looked peaceful. The aide noticed her face had become unlined—the skin smooth as if the world had never touched her with care. Katja's hand was cold now too.

The rocking has quickened and I am sinking. I must throw off every counterweight if I'm to rocket up through this space and out. I'm down to the last bit of ballast, the hardest to shift. But there it is over the edge. "Forgive me" is falling away.

"Lu, I have supper ready," Jon called as he heard the door unlock.

"I'm starving," she called back. She hung her coat over the back of a chair in the kitchen. Her eye fell on the envelope Jon had propped against her glass. Lucia picked it up and, reading the address, walked over to Jon by the stove, dumping it casually in the trash on her way to him. "What's cookin'?" She asked brightly. He turned away from Lucia.

"Pasta," he said, trying to match her tone.

After they boarded, Jon slipped his hand down the side of his computer case before stowing it under the seat ahead. His fingertips graze the envelope he'd retrieved in a hurry as they were leaving. Later, he thought he might draw out the letter, insisting they open it together. But Lucia had taken a tranquilizer. As the engines roared for take off, she adjusted her pillow.

Briefly, the aide examined Katja's hand, absorbed by its morbid hue. Suddenly, she felt a change and saw Katja's chest rise in a breath followed by too long a pause. The young woman felt her own heart speed up. It knocked against her chest. She observed a further breath. Then, again, too long without another. Oh my god, am I watching death? No. One more gentle intake. So gentle. Then. Yes. Stillness.

Lucia was out cold. Later, she would attribute the clarity of her dream to the drug.

She dreamed she was a child in a room she remembered. A large man's hands were holding her around the waist, the reek of vodka warming the back of her neck. His voice was booming but she could not make out the words. A fragile blond woman was ignoring this man as she placed a wreath on Lucia's head. In the dream, Lucia knew the wreath could harm her. She opened her mouth to say so. The woman reached toward her without listening to her. She had a match in her hands. Lucia realized the woman was going to light candles on the wreath even though the man's hands shook with laughter and drink. Time stopped and Lucia was suspended in a state of terror. Then, she felt a surge of tenderness from the woman enter her in a new way. Lucia opened her mouth to scream but, instead, lifted by transmitted power, she rose into space. She was able to spin around and shout defiantly at the man. His fingers release her as she lifted off, a release total as death, while he shrank away from her voice like smoke.

The travelers stood by the front desk of their hotel. Jon, who had barely slept on the flight, accepted a few tourist materials from the concierge. He had not tampered with the envelope even with Lucia deeply asleep beside him, preferring to wait for joint discovery. He felt increasingly sure it contained news and that she had received these messages before. Lucia, by contrast, wanted only to gain their room to change and head out. She was alive with energy.

Susanna sat in front of her light box in a much nicer apartment than she had been used to. Over the past months, she had been able to keep her work hours, without fail, had been able to purchase the light box and had moved. She'd dropped her married name with its terrifying associations and was Susanna Erikson again. She closed her eyes and turned the box on. As soon as the light bathed her, Susanna felt a surge of tenderness as strong as a magnet directing a compass needle. It righted her like a steady-cam.

At a table in a small restaurant near *Gamla Stan*, Lucia translated from the menu for Jon. She had allowed him a half hour nap before dinner so Jon was feeling revived. They toasted each other. Jon opened the tourist brochure with Swedish festivals and folklore. He flipped to the page describing the events that would begin in the morning. He began to read aloud. Lucia laughed, almost giddy. Jon began to fuss with his plate but she took his hand aside and lifted his fork to feed him. He had never seen her quite so uninhibited, so child-like. Her eyes were illuminated. Now, it wasn't her pupils that looked fathomless. The very blue of her eyes seemed boundless. They freed him. He would not bring up the letter. He would throw it out. This was not a laboratory. A sensual pleasure circled through Jon. What use were histories when this new story was being written? Lucia leaned toward him and gently put her hand over his, closing the booklet.

"Tomorrow, we will see children dressed as witches in bright skirts and headscarves. They will run about, hoping for sweets in exchange for their art works."

"Do you remember this from childhood?" Jon asked.

Lucia shook her head. "I remember very little. But I do know where the witches are heading."

"Where?"

"They fly to *Blåkulla*, Blue Mountain, to meet the devil.

Blood Sport

Where are you?

The balls blink in their short sequence. Mars is typing.

forum

Cobblestones make the bus lurch. Bracing herself with her feet, Claudia's thumbs tap out her message.

Great! Meet you in an hour!

k

At the Colosseum.

k l8r

That's 12:30.

ik

It takes Claudia a moment to translate ik. She sends back a string of cheery emoji. How did parents communicate with their teens before texting? She wishes Marissa, who she calls Mars, used punctuation. Wishes they all did. The habit of leaving off periods bothers her particularly. The last time this came up, Mars said, pointing, "Mom, totally unnecessary. *Everything has its own speech bubble.*" Claudia was shocked she'd never focused on this graphic but it didn't matter, one shouldn't mess with grammar.

This morning, content to sit in a café and have another espresso, she let Marissa leave the hostel by herself with the tour group. She was unsure about this—neither of them were experienced travelers—but it was their third and last day in Rome. Mars was persuasive—she was going to be sixteen in another couple months—the tour guide was reassuring and Claudia had the tiniest hangover. Tiny. That extra glass of wine last night. Well, when in Rome . . .

Claudia has taken the bus to meet up with Mars. With a firm grip on the pole, she watches the Eternal City out the bouncing windows. They are on to Florence after this. Traveling up the boot.

Getting off, Claudia takes the right hand turn in front of a set of steep stairs. Consulting her map, she starts on the road that leads to the road that leads directly to the Colosseum. Or so she thinks. But when she arrives at the next intersection, the road name is wrong. She asks another tourist. The man is Dutch and very accommodating. For all his willingness to give her advice, she realizes he is unsure himself. She likes his accent so she allows him to bend over her map for a few minutes, with his wispy hair. Thanking him, Claudia heads off again until she thinks he can no longer see her. She consults her map a second time. Her map—it came inside her guidebook—is not at scale to show all the street names. Claudia feels an itch start up behind one ear. She forces herself not to scratch. Instead, she slides her finger across the map surface, scouting the streets around her. Finally, she spots an intersection on the map she believes to be the one she can just see several blocks ahead. This is the right area. She is sure even if her Dutch gentleman is not.

Claudia begins gamely toward the intersection. She walks faster than is absolutely comfortable. She catches herself and reminds herself to take in and enjoy the pines shading the walls on her left and, at a distance, their same tall profiles and beautiful canopies on her right. Umbrella pines, she thinks. She teaches her fifth graders to observe closely. She teaches them this is the basis of scientific discovery.

Even though it's early spring, the day is becoming hot. Claudia regrets her long sleeves. And why hadn't she worn flats? On top of which, the intersection looks no closer. The itching behind her ear intensifies. Hives? Claudia does a mental review of possible allergens. She stops to rummage around her bag for Benadryl. Having located a packet, she decides to wait to see if the symptoms progress. Maybe it is nothing. She would hate to be sleepy for no reason.

Her self-talk is interrupted by the background worry she has been trying not to have. What if she doesn't reach Mars before the rest of the group heads into the Colosseum? Surely, the tour guide won't leave her alone outside? Claudia desperately wishes she had had a clear conversation with the guide about this eventuality. Damn it. And the guidebook mentioned pickpockets. Claudia breathes in sharply and retires the idea. She won't dilly dally to text again. She will make it there before there is any problem.

Finally, finally she is at the intersection. She looks up the broad street for the Colosseum. It has been about twenty minutes since she stepped off the bus. A steady stream of traffic glistens in the sun. Where is the iconic edifice? No building looks even familiar.

"Crap," she says out loud. She realizes she is allowing herself to be vulgar in a way she never would at home. A bead of anxiety rolls around her stomach. It rolls and ruptures, washing the lining with acid. She puts her hand over her stomach, reaches into her bag for her phone and texts Marissa.

Where are you now?

forum

I am close but can't see the Colosseum yet.

There is a pause before Marissa responds.

r u lost

I don't think so.

turn on maps!!!!!

The string of exclamation points makes Claudia smile. Finally, punctuation. Despite the expense, she does as Marissa orders. Turning on the Internet, she instantly sees her mistake. She should have turned left at the outset. Now, she is skirting the entire Palatine Hill. Given her mistake, she is still all right. Thank goodness she'd left an entire hour to make this part on foot. Claudia memorizes the remaining route and turns roaming back off. She starts off at a faster clip.

Oriented, she feels a rush of pleasure. She is very hot but her blood is moving. The dullness of the wine has lifted. She swings her arms briskly as she walks. Claudia doesn't remind herself to notice the sunlight. She sees everything. Ahead on the left, an old woman stoops over a green patch between two walls. The woman is collecting something from the neglected grass. Claudia notes the patterned pouch slung from her shoulder around her waist. It is full of some leaf. Claudia watches with interest how quickly the woman cuts the plant at the base and stows it.

Claudia pauses to text Mars. It has just come to her as she watches the old peasant that she will pass the Palatine Hill entrance. This will be a good place to meet up. She imagines Mars with her sunny smile coming through an ornamented gate. Robert is wrong about Claudia always living on the surface of things. He is wrong.

Looking up, Claudia notes a young man has approached the woman. He is nineteen or twenty, she guesses. Judging by his clothes, he is American. His boots, standard campus wear, are basic but expensive. Ditto his hoodie. Every item bland. Normcore is not—from her brief experience and observation— a European thing.

The boy bends down to speak to the woman. She turns a gap-toothed grin up to him. She shows him the plant she is foraging. He takes a leaf and, without hesitation, eats it. His back is to Claudia so she doesn't see his smile until he turns away from the woman and starts back toward the street. He gives the woman a thumbs-up as he departs. The squat woman waves back with her stubby knife.

The young man has a sweet face, a gleaming smile in a scruffy beard.

Claudia is almost abreast of the neglected patch. She shifts her course to come closer to the woman, curious to see if she can identify what the woman is collecting. Claudia has become quite a gardener since Robert left. They stopped attending to the outside of their home some time before he took off—their garden beds neglected in lockstep with the slow desertion of their marital bed. That was twenty years ruined.

She watches the woman stoop over and cut the plant. She can tell, now that she is close, the woman is Roma. Just because Robert is the ethnologist, doesn't mean she, Claudia, is culturally illiterate. With Claudia's eyes on her, the gypsy rotates her head and looks directly back. Her eyes are dark but with a cataract bluish center, reflective as an old pet's. Claudia realizes the woman is collecting sorrel. The squalor of the little patch is evident now. Claudia shudders to think the boy has eaten something directly from it, no better than eating off the street. Dogs pee in there. She slows as she passes the gypsy. The woman's condition makes Claudia uncomfortable—rooting around for food like this. They do not exchange smiles. Claudia thinks of the pickpockets.

All at once, Claudia is swept outside herself by the savage noise of a collision. Metal pops and squeals. Claudia whips her head around as a white scooter jumps the curb just feet in front of her. She springs back and collides with the Roma woman. They fall together. Without thinking, Claudia scrambles up, pushing herself against the older woman. Once upright, she turns guiltily to help the gypsy. But the woman is already up on her short legs, waving a fist and yelling into the traffic. Claudia looks over to the driver of the scooter who is pinned by his bike to the sorrel. Blood drips down his face from his hairline. He manages to sit up. He comes to his feet as Claudia reaches him and begins immediately to also wave an angry fist and yell toward the street. Traffic is fouling up around the damaged car stopped in the roadway. The motorist's hood is smashed in. He stands beside his car, gesticulating and shouting back at the other man. Claudia doesn't know who is at fault. She remembers Robert's stories of accidents in Calcutta where the drivers flee for fear of being torn limb from limb by the angry mob.

There is honking and yelling in all directions. Voices gain in pitch and volume. No one seems interested in Claudia. She glances over at the gypsy. The woman is quiet now. She stands watching the dispute with her hands on her hips, her blue-hazed eyes squinting. Claudia tries to apologize. She says, "Mi dispiace," in the direction of the woman but not loudly enough to be heard. She is frightened of further involvement and delay. The window of Mars's safe supervision is closing. Claudia doesn't really speak Italian anyway. What use can she possibly be? She didn't even see what happened. Brushing herself off and turning away, she starts back down the Via dei Cerchi.

Large stains of sweat make her shirt cling under her arms and between her shoulder blades. She shifts her bag to her other shoulder and shakes her shoulders up and down to loosen her shirt. In the moment of slowing to make this small movement, the man from the scooter reaches her. He raps forcefully on her back. Startled, Claudia turns to face him. The man speaks explosively, jabbing his finger back toward the scene of the accident, now five or six yards behind them. Claudia's heart races, watching his bloodied face contort in anger. It is imperative she communicate she cannot help his cause.

"Non parlo Italiano," she says with all the elegance of someone who has a few phrases from a phrase book.

This neither convinces nor dissuades him. Claudia feels panic begin to rise. He has not touched her, beyond the tap, but he is very exercised. At any moment he might grab hold of her to keep her in place as a witness. Claudia thinks she feels a violent possibility coming off him like the shimmer from a mirage. Beyond his shoulder she sees his scooter in the grass, its front end torqued. Then, she sees the other driver storming toward them. The air fills with the mournful wave-like cry of European sirens approaching, a sound she associates with old war films.

"I can't help you. I did not see what happened." She closes her eyes and waves her hands from her closed eyes to the crash scene.

Then, while repeating this sign language, she also shakes her head, "No," from side to side. With ever more animated gestures, he keeps right on speaking at her. If the police reach them, the situation will become impossible. Mars will be stranded alone in a foreign city. Claudia has Mars's ticket for admission to the Colosseum. She now feels certain the tour guide will lose patience and leave Mars outside to wait for her mother.

With a rushed stride, the other driver catches up to them and reaches for the scooter driver. The scooter driver snaps around to confront him. The physical threat Claudia imagined is now close at hand. Claudia does not stay to watch it unfold. Seeing her chance, she bolts. Behind her, the noise mounts. There are more voices and the siren drawing closer. She stops just long enough to slip off her heeled sandals. Barefoot, she runs like she hasn't in decades. Almost as if she is Mars's age. Along the sidewalk, people step aside. From the corner of her eye, she catches a few of them turning to watch her as she flies past. Claudia cannot tell if the noise is keeping up with her. The hot air burns her lungs. Her legs hurt. Then, with another burst, she is sure the cacophony is falling off behind her. Claudia glances back over her shoulder. The men have returned to the scene of the accident. No battle seems to have taken place. The police car is stopped there.

She stops. She puts on her sandals and runs her hand through her tangled hair. Still shaking, she moves close to the wall to be as inconspicuous as possible and leans against it to catch her breath. As soon as she can, she continues to the corner where she finds herself at the Piazza. There is the Via di San Gregorio. Going around the corner to the left, she can no longer be seen, even if someone is still looking for her. She puts her hand to her pounding heart. Her shirt is soaked through. Claudia lifts her gaze. The road ahead rises slightly and then dips down again. Beyond it she sees the familiar contours of the walls of the great amphitheater.

"Thank god," whispers Claudia, although she believes in no deity. A self-deprecating smile blooms on her lips—it is truly all going to be all right—as she puts her hand in her bag to retrieve her phone. She will text Mars how close she is. She walks as she does this. Her bag has a number of zippered pockets. The little one, where she keeps her phone, is open. Reaching in, she is so abuzz with relieved satisfaction that it takes a moment to register the phone is gone. Claudia comes to a complete stop and searches every corner of her bag. Had she failed to close the pocket and lost the phone in the fall? Had the gypsy lifted it?

As these questions, and others, race through her mind, she sprints for the gates. She is now effectively cut off from Mars. It has become a matter of chance if Mars will come out at the appointed place, at the appointed time. She curses their dependence on their phones. She does not stop to take off her sandals, she does not notice her legs, or her lungs. She is practically airborne, spirited along by maternal anguish.

Fortunately, the Palatine Gates are not far. A crowd is entering, exiting, and milling about. Vendors hock trinkets. Claudia reaches them and scans the crowd for Mars's golden head. She spies a blond, bending over to tie a sneaker, near the gates. When the girl stands, it is some other kid. Claudia looks around madly. She cannot think what to do. Five full minutes creep by. Claudia descends into states of distress unknown to her. With her soaking blouse glued to her torso, half un-tucked, and her hair wild, tourists eye her sideways as they pass.

Once, when Mars was little, Claudia had taken her to a big

department store. For a few minutes only, she'd been distracted and Mars had toddled off. There had been a handful of seconds of free fall before she'd seen Mars' feet under a near-by rack of clothes. That was the closest she'd ever been to this, and it had been a matter of minutes, years ago.

How had she let this happen? Claudia begins to bargain with the god she doesn't believe in. She promises to pay more attention, to pay more attention to everything, to grow up.

Another ten minutes pass and there is still no sign. Claudia's thoughts are becoming disordered. The hostel seems a possible place to go for help. They would have contact information for the tour guide. Or the police. Even in her panic, Claudia realizes fifteen minutes is too soon to report someone missing.

"Come out, Mars. Come out." Her lips tremble. A hand touches her elbow. Claudia glances over into a worried young face.

"Are you all right?"

"No. My daughter is supposed to meet me here but I've lost my cell phone and she isn't here."

The young man reaches into his pocket. "Use mine."

Claudia grabs at the phone. "Oh my god. Thank you." She tries not to burst into tears. Frantically, she makes a new message and hits send.

> Sweetheart, where are you? I am outside the Palatine Gates.

Claudia watches the phone in her hand. It stares back at her, unchanging. Claudia looks at the young man. She looks back at the blank phone. Then, as if moved by the magic of fairytales the balls begin their dance. Mars is typing. Claudia clutches the front of the young man's shirt.

whose phone u got

Doesn't matter! Where are you?!!!

The young man accepts Claudia's awkward grip and smiles broadly, happy to have helped. Her tears can no longer be restrained. There is another delay. It goes on a beat too long. Claudia lets go of the young man. Then, the balls begin to flash.

colesseum

Why?

you didn't return text i went to join group

Are you with them now?

no they r inside

Where EXACTLY are you?

Marissa gives her coordinates.

Don't move! I'm coming!

Claudia looks up at the young man.
"She is at the Colosseum."
"Then, let's go. I'm going anyway," says the young man. Claudia looks at him with infinite gratitude. Claudia wants to run but keeps herself to a brisk step. The youth keeps up effortlessly. During their walk, Claudia asks the young man's name. He tells her he is Ben. It is then she sees, with a start, he is the kid who'd eaten the gypsy's dirty leaf. Claudia doesn't mention this. They do not speak further. She is walking too fast anyway.

On their arrival, Ben points to the gate where Mars is waiting. There is a crowd there, too, and Claudia can't see Marissa among them. Ben's phone buzzes. He stops to read the message and shows it to Claudia.

icu

Claudia looks up and there is Mars standing at the edge of a group, smiling and unconcerned. Her child. Claudia gives a moan, wipes her sleeve across her nose, and runs to Mars. Ben watches the reunion as Mars hugs her mom. Even from a few feet away, he can see Claudia grips her too hard. Marissa pulls back, having felt her mother's wet shirt.

"What happened to your phone, Mom?"

"I dropped it, maybe. There was an accident. It is all sort of complicated." Ben meanders up to them.

"You look insane," says Mars. Ben laughs.

"Mars, this is Ben. Ben this is Marissa."

"Hey," says Ben.

"He loaned me his phone."

"Thanks," says Mars.

"No worries," says Ben breaking into his stunning smile.

"She doesn't normally look like a lunatic," says Mars returning to the topic of her mother.

"Mars!" says Claudia.

"Well, you don't."

"I was just really scared."

"Well, I was fine and we're all together now," says Mars, circling her finger to indicate the three of them and smiling back at Ben.

The waiting and crowds are a bother in the heat. However, once inside, Claudia becomes excited. They climb up to the second floor. They wander the perimeter with Ben stopping to read from placards. Claudia is thrilled to be with her daughter at this ancient site. Under Marssia's guidance, they find a spot, at a rail, quite alone, with a spectacular view across the entire stadium. The perforated walls encircle them, rising high against a cobalt sky.

Claudia looks down. There below are the remains of the subterranean passageways where beasts had been lifted by hoists to the slaughter, thousands of them—deer, lions, crocodiles, and ostrich. And men thrown to lions or bears to be torn apart like the Calcutta drivers. From the hot sand, she senses rising up shades of the single-handed combat with the crowd cheering or calling for death around her. Claudia feels queasy. This taste for blood. Her guidebook says, "Legend has it that as long as the Colosseum stands, Rome will stand; and when Rome falls, so will the world." Her head swims. She pictures gladiators, slaves, and criminals. She imagines their fates. Centuries and centuries of violence. Even now, children running into crowds with bombs strapped to their narrow chests.

Claudia looks over at Ben chatting with Mars. He rescued her from terror. He befriended a person who foraged greens from vacant lots.

Marissa is beaming back at Ben's smile there on the edge of a ruin.

First Task

Jeremy caught the C at 14th Street after a boisterous night reconnecting with friends in Bushwick. He jiggles his right foot over his left knee. He is going to bite the bullet because, back in town for the week, the tall buildings no longer remind him of soaring prospects but of possible shortfalls.

Thinking of this, he looks across the train at a black boy, of four or five, with huge eyes, also squirming in his seat. He is playing with a plastic truck. A girl beside the boy sits up tall, reading her book, ignoring her brother's wiggling. The book and the truck, their clean faces and their absorption are telling. Jeremy's gaze settles on the mom who takes care of her young. She appears to be mixed race, regal and weary. She probably struggled up. Maybe is still struggling. Jeremy looks back at the small boy's hands exploring his truck. His active fingers, fired by interest and an open-ended story, are moving with the flight of an artist. Jeremy breathes through tightness in his chest. He knows this gift will be stolen.

He does not intend to shift his attention from what is too often snatched away in the cradle, but finds himself on a different well-worn thought thread. He reverts to his idée fixe—that he, Jeremy, is pinned on his back, like Kafka's cockroach, by a heavy exoskeleton. It's not the Jeremy part but the Gavin Lodge parts of his name that weigh on him—resonant as they are of family connections. He wants to break free. Jeremy has ceased entirely to think about the boy across from him who, on his father's side, had great grandparents whose hands were shackled.

Jeremy Gavin Lodge's name is a problem he carts around. It consigns him to correct generations of squandered talents. These talents, unlike the boy's that may not stand a chance, should have been secured by fortune. But they were not. The advantage was in his family's court because they arrived early and grabbed it. However, with spooky regularity, promising deals—matrimonial and financial—went belly up. Family lore had it there was a fatal sunniness that prospered during the gilded age of capitalism but barely glimmered through the Great Depression.

Jeremy is cued by the positional adjustments between cars, metal scraping metal, and the thud of air from the brakes. The train is pulling into the 96th street station. He rises from his seat and hangs from the pole, waiting for the door to open.

From the age of eighteen to twenty-one, Jeremy attended one of the universities in operation since his forbearers were building railroads. He strategically pursued a double major in finance and filmmaking. He could "see with his eyes closed" as his voluble father used to say—a natural at thinking in pictures. Same with funding-raising. A natural. Such an "essential piece of movie making" as his mother would say.

With a bing-bong, the first note higher than the second, the doors slide open. A surprising number of incoming passengers block Jeremy's exit. He does not want to miss his stop or be caught by the closing door. Looking sharp, he shifts around the flow, saying, "getting off," as he pushes past the boarding passengers. Even this ritual, with its low-grade anxiety, is familiar to him from boyhood. In its old rhythms and sway, it gives him a deep bodily comfort fundamental as oatmeal.

When he graduated, there were years of steady progress in L.A. Jeremy built contacts, was hired on projects, moved into directing and producing. His considerable kinetic charm and his pedigree greased the wheels. Then, a year ago, at thirty, just as he was posed to truly launch, there had been a spectacular failure of a picture. It almost sucked dry what means remained to him. Like those historic personal reversals in the family, it was an ugly collapse of everyone's expectations. Jeremy, nearly broke, spent weeks with the blinds drawn, rarely stirring from his bungalow into the perpetually sunshine. Looking back, he saw there'd been excessive optimism. He'd gotten a lot of people in trouble.

As February began to lift, he turned thirty-one. Common sense finally drew him out. He dusted off his school connections and found a day job, an entry-level spot at a P.R. firm, run by an alum. As he slogged his way through the days, ideas began to percolate again. One of these took shape and, with it, Jeremy experienced a returning tide of animation. He decided to take his filmmaking network and grasp of dramatic effects into manufacture. It would require money for start-up but nothing like the budget of even a small picture.

Jeremy leaves the subway station, surrounded by others climbing with him. Gum or gurry in constellations of flattened dark circles mark each stair in his progress to the street. He notices the patterning. Buddhists see beauty even in filth. The little boy from the train scrambles past, grazing Jeremy with those nimble fingers. One step ahead, the child moves too far to the middle. A tall businessman, rushing for a train, knocks into the five-year-old without even noticing. The boy stands for a few seconds but has lost his balance. He tips backward. Jeremy lunges for and catches him. A vivid image flashes through Jeremy of the child's head splitting open as it meets the stairs and the youngster tumbling to his death. He steadies the child whose mother presses up from behind and assumes her son's weight. She holds him, making sure he is stable, then steps next to him, takes his hand and, without breaking her stride to look back at the stranger who is part of the rescue, gains the rest of the stairs with both children in tow. She is practiced at dodging what the world hurls at her kids.

Although Jeremy's heart is still racing, he looks down again at the stairs. He allows their surface to enter his eyes. The grimy cement flavors his rumination. He tries to let go his obsession with opportunities missed despite privilege. He knows in a global way but strives to know, now, at the cellular level of the pavement—a ground over which rising hordes have left their stain—how every achievement in his life has been made easy for him.

In L.A., at night, before this trip, he worked on sketches for a product. He felt sure he'd hit on something that would take off, combining, as it did, novelty with the tried and true. Why he thought success likely was simple. His uncanny ability to see a story in development, from a brief description, made it possible to visualize a pathway to market lift-off. He looked into materials, methods, and similar products. He hired a set-designer to take his sketches to a finished stage. He guarded the drawings closely. Eventually, he would need the help of creative engineers and model makers. But this was Hollywood. They would be easy to find. It did not matter the gizmo would be a trivial thing no one needed.

"The project is a creative re-visioning of things that sparked my fancy as a boy. It is a kind of toy," he told potential investors, whetting their interest without giving anything away.

A proof-of-concept model will be needed and prototypes to rope them in, things for which he lacks resources. Now, walking up Central Park West, his and Edith's alienation years behind him, he is hoping for an injection of funds from his chilly mother. The bullet he must bite.

A breeze blows east, carrying a few white blossoms from the park—Pear? Hawthorn? They are confections tumbling at his feet. But spring's flowers fade. Also dynasties. Jeremy watches a young man's shoulders in his jacket as he passes on his left, his hips tipping from side to side in his jeans. Another warm gust brings a scent of spring and sweeps the fallen flowers further along. Jeremy feels a pleasurable itch. Youth departs, too, but maybe not yet.

"It's me, Mum. Jeremy," he says into the speaker. He waits for her answer but there is none, just a pause, then the buzzer going off to buzz him in. When the elevator arrives at the eighth floor, he breathes in the hallway. The musty odor is as familiar as the maroon carpeting and the dark walls framing a few potted plants busy dying by a hall window. Jeremy believes these same plants have been failing to thrive since 1993. He knocks on his mother's door.

Always thin and tall, she is thinner now.

"You stopped dyeing your hair," he says, spooked.

"Hello to you, too," says his mother.

And there we are, thinks Jeremy, taking no responsibility, like the flowers in the street blown out of reach by an unseen force.

"You look wonderful," he lies, stepping forward to kiss her cheek.

"Yes, well, good to see you," Edith says. "Come in, come in . . ."

Jeremy steps through into the spacious apartment. Light filters in from the street. It is reflected off the building opposite and in through the large windows with their transparent panels. The rooms are spotless. Jeremy's eye takes in the top of the sideboard in the dining room with its polished silver candlesticks and bowls. Does she have someone help with the cleaning? Probably not. Edith, careful with money, might be more careful now, having retired from teaching. He does not know what his father left her beyond the apartment.

Jeremy also does not know the terms of Edith's will, if the apartment will come to him, or his sister, Corinna, or be left for both of them. He does not know if it will be left in trust or if they will be free to sell. Obviously, he is hoping. Nina has wondered this point with him. They will go for drinks after this.

Looking at his mother with her pearls, Jeremy remembers a picture of her from the late fifties, dressed as a Greek warrior for a school event. She is about seven in the photo. She stands in profile, wearing a tunic and laced sandals, brandishing a hand-painted shield. The shield and sword are her handiwork. She is pointing her sword heavenward. She leads him to a seat in the living room, where tea is laid out, with the same unyielding posture.

"Edith," says Jeremy, as they settle for tea, "how are you?"

"Call me Mother, Jeremy, please." He shifts in his seat. He instructs himself to humor her. She hands him a teacup, steaming with a floral blend. Jasmine he thinks from the perfume. There is a new book on the coffee table with the title, *Amazona*. It has a striking green bird on the cover. There is a second book beneath on Costa Rica. He takes a sip of tea. It is Jasmine.

"Planning a trip, Mum?" He points his teacup at the books on the table.

"Hm?" says Edith. She looks distracted or absent for a moment. "No. Here, have a cookie." She passes a plate of shortbread to him. He takes one and looks at his mother. It's not just that she's thinner. Her eyes are red rimmed. Despite the marked differences between his parents, he is sure she loved his father, even his girth and volume. However, her tears at the funeral had been constrained. So it can't be crying now. Her lids must be a condition of some kind. He makes a mental note to ask Nina if she knows. Funny how you can spend three years without seeing a parent and care immediately, on seeing them, about the details of their health. He does not plumb the depths of what kind of care this is.

"I'm fine," says Edith.

Once he has the cookie wedged in his mouth, she asks, "Tell me about the new job; how is it?" Here, her voice travels upward with a suggestion of suspense. Jeremy and Edith do not speak directly of money so she doesn't know how badly his finances have been hit. She guesses. When he'd started in pictures, she'd been gung-ho, despite the difficulties between them. But then, as the years past, more true to form, she increasingly insisted she did not know how these indie projects would "lead anywhere." Jeremy could never convince her they were already somewhere, though, in fairness, he found it was not unreasonable for her, once he was investing in projects, to be concerned he'd lose his shirt. It irritated him but he understood.

Then, he did lose his shirt. He imagines she blames the family curse. So Jeremy is truthful about the limits of the new P.R. job. He does not paint a falsely upbeat picture. Lines of disappointment accumulate around her eyes. He does not tell her, straight off, about his invention.

She'd had a bad flu at the end of the winter. Now, she is trying to put on weight. This news, that she is frail, does not land. Jeremy watches her hands. They have always been her most expressive feature. They are not particularly interesting hands but the gestures she makes with them are. She moves them with graceful, slow, open-palmed motions. The hands come toward her chest. Her fingertips touch her breastbone and then she turns them outward, with the palms up, and sweeps them down, in arcs, punctuating her words. Sometimes she rotates her hands with a faint "float-wave," rocking the hand back and forth while she speaks. It is as if she were conducting under water. When she isn't speaking, her hands rest quietly in her lap. As a little boy, those still hands signaled Jeremy that he was being heard.

Now, her hands are moving as she chats about the weather, Nina, and her friends. He waits for her hands to settle in her lap. He leans forward.

"Mum, I have another project I'm working on."

"Another film?" she asks warily.

"No. This is a product design. A toy."

"A toy?"

"Well, not really for children. It is somewhere between a toy and a desk ornament. A curio."

He sees Edith endeavor not to let the first thing in her head come out of her mouth. She looks at her son, leaning forward, his great head jutting toward her. He turns it like a gem in a jeweler's hands, a faceted thing made to catch the light. He is even better looking with age.

"A curio? Didn't you just lose a great deal on that film?"

Jeremy winces.

"I don't mean to sound discouraging, darling."

He does not answer. He lets her calling him "darling" sink in. He recognizes it for what it is, a willed evocation of his childhood. He decides this isn't a terrible segue.

"Remember what I liked as a kid?"

"You were always such a restless, busy child. You liked a lot of things. Typography?"

"Before that."

"Um, photography? Drawing?"

"Before that."

"Oh. Let me think." She goes quiet for a moment. "Entomology?"

"Yes. And, in particular, Coleoptera," he says, enunciating it with a little too much force.

"What is that again?"

"Beetles."

"Yes?" asks Edith.

"Well, I have designed a snow globe that is also a project." She cannot help but look alarmed. Is she thinking this is too ambitious a departure or that it does not sound like him? Rather than hoping the whimsy of the project will catch her interest, Jeremy focuses on its drama. He has this.

"What do you mean?"

"I can describe it but I'd rather show you. I have photos of the drawings on my phone. Come," he says patting the seat beside him. He makes his voice as warm as possible. Edith moves next to Jeremy. He remembers to make eye contact, and, smiling, scrolls through the drawings. Little by little, she sits differently. It isn't a huge change. She leans in a little so her torso no longer makes a 90-degree angle with her lap.

On the phone before them are exquisite renderings, made by the set-designer, of large snow globes. Like all snow globes, they present a miniature mis en scène. In this case, it is of insect specimens painted with the detail of an Audubon print, displayed on twigs, or rocks, or leaves that are also beautifully represented. One specimen per globe, six in the series. The globes sit on a metallic base with the Latin name of the beetle on it.

"These are wonderful drawings."

"Aren't they? I had a set-designer do them for me," says Jeremy. Edith pulls back toward center. Is it the expense? Jeremy remembers not to second-guess her.

On top of each globe is an ornate handle. The toys have a steamer punk look—their nineteenth century vibe also of the moment. Jeremy explains that the "snow" inside will be made of thin flakes of gold metal, light enough to swirl. The flakes are stamped into letterforms. Each globe in the line contains all the letters of the Latin name of the bug. When you shake the globe, they circle around and settle in no particular order. The magic of the gizmo is contained in the curious handle on top. By pressing various buttons on the handle you make a tweezer descend on a rigid arm. Mimicking the carnival game, but with a sci-fi look, you can use this grappler, manipulating the handle, to gather the fallen letters one at a time. It is a challenging task. Each insect has its name embossed on its body. When the player succeeds in placing the right gold letters into these indentations, the base produces a whirring sound and the beetle lights up. The liquid is designed to amplify the light so the whole globe glows. At any point the player can restart the game by shaking loose the letters or just leave the letters in place, telescope up the pincer until it is concealed again in the handle, and use the globe as a light, operating it from a touch-switch on the base. This particular feature pleases Jeremy. He designed the switch to work only after the beetle is unlocked by its name.

Jeremy patiently explains all of this. Edith's hands stay still in her lap throughout. When he is done, she looks over at him; her steel colored eyes are hard to read. Her lips part as she exhales.

"Adam's task." Then a single further word escapes in a whisper: "darling."

It is a little over an hour later when Jeremy meets Nina at the bar. There she is, his almost twin, his adored sister, Corinna, with her silver hair. The siblings laugh as they embrace each other.

"It has been too long," exclaims Nina, although she brought her family out to L.A. just six months ago.

"Is Oscar with the kids?" asks Jeremy.

Nina nods and signals the bartender.

"Aren't you trendy with that hair." Nina had told him about dyeing it but he hadn't remembered.

"I know." She tosses her head, showing it off. "And how did it go with Mum?"

"Difficult to say. There were some good bits. She called me "darling.""

"Get out," Nina inhales, astonished.

Jeremy crosses his heart with his finger. "Twice. The first time, I was freaking her out and she was trying to cover by being nice. The second time was so quiet, I almost couldn't hear her."

"How nice was she?"

"She offered to call Uncle Alan in Chicago."

"That *is* nice."

"Yeah, and she also said, once the prototypes were made, there were some people she could talk to. I explained that at this stage I didn't need much, about a hundred thousand."

"That seems a fuck of a lot."

"Well, there are technical hurdles. I need to hire people. It's all about the margins, getting the cost of manufacture as low as possible without sacrificing the look or feel. And getting the mechanics right."

"Listen to you, Captain of Industry."

"Yeah, well." He pauses while they drink. "I'm stoked. I've found a firm I like, but they aren't cheap."

"What kind of firm?"

"A place that does product design."

"Maybe we're wrong to think Mum has funds to spare?"

Jeremy shakes his head. "Who even knows what she has?"

"On the other hand, she has to be living on something. There are things that turn up still—not like the Hermès scarves she has always had—which were not bought on a teacher's wages."

As the cocktails arrive, the two fall into a favorite topic—the mystery of the family wealth. All their lives, they had heard of the colossal spendthrifts of the past, they were warned about them, about high spirits and poor judgment, but they were raised in ignorance of their family's remaining holdings. Their guesswork gains momentum with their drinks. Although the family talked as if strained, there had always seemed to be plenty. They remember how their father had hinted at an inheritance. He had been very generous with them while he was alive, paying all their expenses growing up, and while at school, and then giving them each a sum on graduation to "get set up." His parents, they knew, had given the apartment to him. There was money. Oh, yes, there was money. The siblings shook their heads. The question was how much? After their dad died everything went to their mother. And Edith did not speak of such things. They laugh about what it would take to pry it out of her. Neither refers directly to what happened between Jeremy, Nina, and Edith years before their father's death. Why Edith froze him out.

"Screw them," says Nina.

"Who?"

"Both of them," she insists. "Dad for not protecting us and Mum for being Mum." Then she pauses. "Anyway, a breakthrough. I mean, her being willing to help at all."

"Yes," says Jeremy, "not what I was hoping for, but a breakthrough." He asks after his three-year-old nephews, who are actual twins. "How are the munchkins?"

"They are unbelievable."

He raises his glass, "Here's to them."

"And to your future."

"Skoal."

They both order another round, one more than they need. It is agreed he will come home with her instead of heading back to Brooklyn. He texts his friends. He wants to see the kids and Nina's handsome Oscar. But first, Nina is eager to share some pot she brought along.

"It's crazy stuff. I never get to smoke any more, since the twins."

"Poor you."

"Don't be mean."

They joke about taking the weed to Edith's apartment to loosen her up but settle on the park. The night air is soft. The streetlights cast silent shadows. Again, Jeremy enjoys the deep contentment of being home in New York. Once they reach the

Spangled Ruin

park, tipsy and full of a renewed sense of promise, Jeremy leads the way along a path to a quiet bench among flowering shrubs.

"What are these," asks Nina as she sits down.

"Azaleas," Jeremy answers.

"Pretty," she says as she leans her own pretty head over her bag to find the stuff.

"How is it you know nothing about nature?" He asks.

"Not a very natural child."

"Hm. What we weren't taught. Could you name any of the tree varieties in Central Park? Black Walnut, Norway Spruce, Dogwood? Or Cherry, of course . . ."

"Of course."

"Or Larch, or Locust . . ."

"You don't need much," she mumbles around the doobie as she lights up, takes a hit, and passes it to him.

"Right, you don't need much," he says through his teeth, imitating a Connecticut lockjaw, "it's about the <u>quality</u>."

After they smoke, Jeremy describes his invention in greater detail than she has previously heard. He makes bigger and bigger gestures as he speaks. She is impressed in a stoned way.

"Kids are gonna love that," Nina breathes, eyes wide.

"It's for adults too."

"Really?"

"That's so ageist of you."

"Wait 'til you've spent some real time around kids. They're not that like us. Dreamier." Nina takes another toke. "No, but seriously, it's all good. There will be science geeks, of every age, that want this thing. You creative genius, you."

"Ah, thanks," he says. Nina pats him on the arm.

Then, he is off again, explaining with great dynamism how this toy "has legs." This unleashes wild mirth. Barely getting themselves under control, Jeremy adds, "You know there are over three hundred thousand kinds of beetle," a little too enthusiastically. Again, they are helpless with laughter. When they settle down, Nina looks at her kid brother.

"Do you know, when you get excited, you wave your hands like Mum? It's kind of a dead give away."

"What?" gasps Jeremy.

"Whaaat?" asks Nina as if she is hearing her voice in an echo chamber.

"That I'm gay?"

"What? Noooo. That you're her son, silly."

"Oh. Sorry." The siblings sit there looking at the shadows of the trees in the breeze. Jeremy realizes he is really high. He watches the shadows dance like his mother's hands or, apparently, his own.

He remembers the afternoon by the lake when he was fifteen. It had been a hot day. That day, too, the trees were waving above them. Nina and he had not planned a swim but could not resist the temptation once on the little private beach, especially since someone had left a towel on a limb to dry. They undressed instantly and ran into the water. Afterward, still naked, they laid side by side on the towel to dry in the sun. Jeremy had just turned over on his stomach and was chatting with his sister, his chin propped on one hand while he gestured with the other, when their mother approached from the cabin. They had been pierced by her voice, high and shrill, as she called his name.

Now, he looks at the night shadows that are almost blue at the edges. A beautiful deep blue. Jeremy wonders if Nina sees the blue. He is about to ask her when Nina sighs as if she has just had a major insight.

"No, no, no, I'm sorry." She slips her arm through his, "Let's walk around a bit." She hauls him up.

They talk about heading to Strawberry Fields, to the Imagine memorial, but neither of them can stay focused long enough to decide if it is too far south or too much trouble. Jeremy tells Nina how his product line is going to be so successful there will be spin-offs, adventure books about early entomologists; and then, maybe, movies based on the books. Down the line, he'll find his way back into the industry. He tells her about the little boy in the subway and how he'd like to get him one of these gizmos when they're made.

"The kid probably has none of the things our lives were padded with."

"Why, because he's black?"

"No. I mean, yes and no. Because, I might have imagined it, but I thought he had a look like he knew necessity."

A little later, under an apple tree in bloom, Jeremy drinks in the fragrance and admits he would like to be in love. With the spring and pot easing stark truths, the siblings pass the apple tree, considering love in its many forms, and come around a dark hedge. In a hallucinogenic second, the bush blows apart. Great chunks break off into three looming fragments. They become human. Silhouettes. Jeremy hasn't yet realized the danger they are in, he is still in the grip of pleasant fantasies, when Nina screams. One of the gang jumps her, putting his hand over her mouth. Jeremy turns to help her but is grabbed by the other two. He makes his best attempt to fight them off. He shakes and twists until he gets one hand free.

Nina has pulled the hand over her mouth away and shouts, "Don't Jeremy," as he tries to land a punch hard enough to make a difference but hears only the slightest sound as his fist slips off the troublemaker's jacket.

Jeremy tries to keep his eyes on Nina. She is wrestling with the man who holds her but Jeremy can't keep her in view. The two who have Jeremy release him only to begin punching him. His field of vision is in swinging slices when he can even open his eyes. At one point, he sees an object, maybe Nina's purse, upside down, being shaken. There is a fall of white squares in the air. He is not aware of the pain but of the immediacy of the powerfully changing moment. On his knees, being hit over and over, he is pleading with them not to hurt Nina when he feels one of the men get hold of his belt. There is a sharp jerk at his waist. He tries to crawl away and is jerked back. He pulls forward and is jerked back again. The burn and bite of the belt sends shocks down his legs. He thinks I am going to be raped. But they are after his wallet. Once this is lifted, one of the men leans down and whispers in his ear, "How much you got, asshole?"

Jeremy feels cold metal against his temple.

"We don't know how much we have," whimpers Jeremy before he is delivered a blow to the head, from whatever the man has in his hand, which sends him sprawling. Then it is quiet.

A full minute passes before Jeremy can pull himself up and look around for Nina. He crawls to his hands and knees and raises his head. He does not see her. His mouth has been scraped raw by the dirt and his head is swimming. With great effort, he gets to his feet.

"Nina," he sputters.

Before he locates her, he feels her hands. She is wrapping her arms in a disorganized way around him, crying into his back.

They stand like that, propping each other up. Jeremy is not finished feeling terrified when tears well up from deep inside him. He is fifteen again, being ordered from the summer cabin because his mother, who used to love him, can't love him any more.

Jeremy turns and takes Nina to his chest, stroking her hair and weeping into it. He pulls her away to look. Nina's hands come to her mouth when she sees his face.

"Jeremy, you're bleeding."

"Did they hit you?"

She shakes her head, no. "I'm all right. But they took Grandma's diamond." Jeremy takes her hand and, shaking with sobs, puts her ring finger to his mouth, then in his mouth. He tastes blood, but whether from where the ring was wrenched off, or his own, he can't tell.

Nina accepts this strange gesture, then pulls him gently off, gathers what she can of their belongings, and gets them started out of the park. Jeremy feels increasingly dizzy and sick. As he moves, pains lacerate his gut. Nina keeps a supporting arm around him but can't move steadily because she is shaking. Despite the tremors, she is driven by the need to find safety.

Oscar parks the sleeping twins with a neighbor. He arrives at the E.D. where Jeremy and Nina are in triage. Nina will be released but Jeremy will be kept over. They have run labs. His wounds have been cleaned but he needs stitches and an abdominal ultrasound. The nurse is chatty in that breezy way of some emergency room nurses. She reassures Oscar. They just want to keep Jeremy under observation until internal bleeding has been ruled out and his heart rate is normal. Most likely, he will be discharged tomorrow. Nina wants to stay with Jeremy but the nurse insists she go home to bed. The nurse explains again to Oscar, because of the alcohol and pot in Nina's system (here she raises an eyebrow) the doctor is reluctant to give Nina something to sleep. But sleep is what his wife needs. There in the close quarters of the curtained enclosure, Oscar kisses Nina all over her face and her bandaged ring finger while the nurse bustles. He moves to the bedside and kisses Jeremy too, less lavishly, on the top of his head, and says they will be back in the morning.

"Do you want someone now? Shall I wake your mother?"

"No," says Jeremy, as the doctor finally appears to close the gash above his eye. "I'll be OK." He looks too pale but the doctor obviously wants them out and Nina must be taken home.

"Com'on, my ratio of a circle's circumference." Oscar, a British mathematician, tucks her under his arm. Nina nods, too tired to object. As she passes his gurney, she takes Jeremy's hand and squeezes it lightly before leaving him to the hospital's care.

The doctor and nurse are reviewing what is on the monitor. The grizzled physician turns to get down to business. He injects Jeremy above the eyebrow and starts to close the wound even before the numbing effect has fully taken. While he works, he asks some questions Jeremy is sure he has already answered multiple times. Jeremy is distracted by the sound of the machines monitoring him.

The doctor finishes with, "What is your pain, now, on a scale of one to ten?"

Jeremy tries to think but he is having trouble. His pain is no longer from separate sites but has become an all-body sensation. For reasons he does not understand, his mouth and brain are not connecting.

"That's OK," says the doctor, nodding to the nurse, "we are going to get you in for that ultrasound then I can get you something to take the edge off. Does that sound good?"

Jeremy's roommate has been thrashing through the night. Between this and the constant interruptions of the nurses, Jeremy has gotten little sleep. Just the pain medicine—whatever it was they fed through his I.V.—has finally allowed him to rest.

"Mum?" he asks when he opens his eyes and sees a long nose lit from the fixture above his bed that has never been switched off. But it is not his mother. It is a resident who comes more fully into the light.

"How are you feeling?"

"What time is it?"

She checks her watch, "Five thirty."

"Better."

"Well, you got pretty banged up but the good news is everything inside looks fine."

"That is good news."

"Your vitals are stable. We'll give you instructions for the contusions and swelling. The stitches will dissolve on their own. We want you quiet for the next few days."

"Here?" asks Jeremy, alarmed.

"No, no. You can be discharged in the morning."

"Isn't it morning now?"

"When the next shift is on. I think they can get you out of here by ten or so. We would like Dr. Somayaji to clear you for take-off."

Jeremy accepts this edict passively. He is way too tired to care. He is just relieved he will be let go.

Then, as the sun comes up and all the nighttime beeping

quiets, Jeremy finally sleeps soundly. When Dr. Somayaji wakes him, mid-morning, a nurse stands by ready to help with discharge. The doctor, a young fellow, tells Jeremy to give his body time to heal before making any big demands of it. He goes over icing the swellings and wound care. He pauses to explore whether Jeremy would like a meeting with the counseling staff before being let go.

"Don't underestimate the effects of being attacked," Somayaji says in a cultivated tone. "You were in shock last night."

"It was awful but I think I'm good," says Jeremy, smiling at the nurse who looks up from the bedside table where she is organizing the forms.

"OK. But don't be brave."

Jeremy looks confused. Somayaji is reflective, as if he is considering. He flashes Jeremy a smile. "I grew up in a rural part of India. A lot of things weren't tolerated there, if you get my drift." The doctor's voice is silken. "I'm a trauma specialist. When we examined you last night, there were skin burns around your waist from your belt. Trauma has a way of triggering earlier traumas. I want to put you on alert to seek help if it does. That's all. OK?"

Jeremy looks into the doctor's green-flecked eyes.

"Gotchu, Doc."

"You live in L.A?"

"That's right, but I have family here."

"Good. You'll be staying with them?"

Jeremy nods.

"Can you take a few days before you fly home?"

"Yes."

"I would advise it. You need anything, you call my service," says Somayaji and hands him his card.

"That's kind of you."

Dr. Somayaji writes out a script and gives it to him.

"This is for pain. It's enough for three days. After that, you should be fine on acetaminophen. Take the extra strength as prescribed. Get sleep. Let your family take care of you." Dr. Somayaji pats Jeremy on the shin, through the hospital blanket, as he turns to go. "The nurse will help you get ready and take you down. Be well, my friend," he says. "Don't be a hero."

"I won't," says Jeremy. Thanks."

Jeremy stays three days with Nina, Oscar, and the twins. The boys are a delight with their piping pronouncements, as long as Nina and Oscar can keep them off him. Ordinary movement excites sharp pains the painkillers don't touch. One rib is cracked. This makes it an agony to laugh. The household, a tinderbox of silliness, is sparked into irrepressible merriment at every turn, precisely because they all know they mustn't be. Even the little boys know. They pull their lips into funny shapes trying not to laugh. Nina's spirits have returned despite purple fingerprints, shading to putty yellow, along both arms. It's a good thing the twins understand the concept of a "boo-boo." Oscar deploys it to keep the toddlers from being too physically affectionate. Oscar is "monstrously diverting" as he says himself. No wonder Nina married him. After some thought, the adult siblings decide not to tell Edith about the mugging. There seems no point.

Dr. Somayaji hovers in the background of discussions about extending Jeremy's stay. Nina teases Jeremy by insisting they can dream up a reason to check in—a suspected infection or, better yet, troubling flashbacks.

"Don't joke about that, Nina, Jesus."

"Oh, don't be such a stiff."

"Forgive me if I have standards."

"What are you two on about?" asks Oscar who has just walked in.

"Jeremy thinks it isn't funny to suggest faking PTSD symptoms just to hear his doctor's voice again."

"Why ever not?" asks Oscar.

The twins burst in, at this point, and Oscar has his hands full restraining them. Conversation shifts abruptly to what might be available, in the kitchen, for good quiet boys at which the twins proclaim, in unison, that they are noisy boys. Oscar and Nina smile at each other as Nina steers the boys toward the door.

"Good things come to noisy boys, too," she says over her shoulder.

Two days later, instead of heeding this advice, Jeremy books his return flight. It costs him something to pull away. He would like to remain in the city that feels like home with the sister who has one.

The cloudlessness of L.A. makes re-acclimation easier than he imagined. His squat stucco house, cool on the inside and not particularly welcoming, reminds Jeremy of the energizing effect of work. His bedroom walls are littered with sketches. These take the sting out of return and his healing wounds. It is not so bad to have come back without a financial commitment. Seeds were sown.

And, in fact, in a little over a week, a note comes in from Uncle Alan. He asks to see the drawings. Several exchanges later, and a check for thirty thousand is on its way. It is a sweetheart deal because Alan, who never had children of his own, built an empire on compasses. What started as a wilderness supply concern evolved into apps for hikers and a web series on navigation aimed at middle-schoolers. Uncle Alan believes in widgets and the buying power of children.

This is the break Jeremy needs. As he knows from funding film, the first investment, once in place, will attract others. In the evenings, Jeremy makes a business plan as airtight as he possibly can. The vulnerability exposed by his injuries and contact with his mother begins to recede even as the weight of the carapace returns. Feeling the old press of his name fuels his impatience to develop this new deal rapidly. At night, he can't sleep. When he does fall off, he often wakes abruptly, covered in sweat, with a dream-twisted version of one of the muggers suffocating him. With daylight, the dreams fade.

Jeremy begins to make the rounds. Thankfully, Hollywood loyalties shift as quickly as the tabloids. Sex scandals, addictions and bad movie deals poison reputations that re-emerge untainted. All it takes is the absolution of a shiny marriage proposal, treatment fad, or hyped project. He knows to avoid those actually burnt by his last film. But he finds takers. The incandescent drawings are persuasive. Every day that sees Jeremy bodily stronger, sees his venture more fully financed. Soon, he will quit his day job to stay on top of the new enterprise. He just isn't there yet. Harried, burning the candle at both ends, Jeremy heads into work. He takes a call without checking the caller.

"Jeremy?" Her voice is unmistakable but different. She sounds nervous.

"Mum is that you? Are you all right?"

"Yes. Yes. I'm so glad I reached you. I have been thinking about your toy." Now, she sounds very bright, more cheerful than he has heard her in ages.

"Really? I've been meaning to call," he fibs. He gathers himself. "Things are moving along quickly. I'm in a strong position thanks to Uncle Alan. I mean, thanks to you for getting him involved. The prototype is being made as we speak," he adds more truthfully.

"What fantastic news. Let me know, darling, when it's ready." Her voice is punchy.

Before Jeremy can answer, he hears the line go dead. He tries to call her back but she doesn't answer. He tries several times. With a bad conscience, he puts his phone away. His tardiness has begun to be noticed on the job. He will call Nina, later, to find out what's up.

Having just hit "send" on several pressing emails, he is trying to make a bull's eye in the mini-dartboard in his cubicle, when the message comes in that Karen, who is senior management, wants to see him. Like Jeremy, Karen is a graduate of the C.E.O.'s alma mater. Vaguely apprehensive, with defenses for any potential lapses forming in his mind, Jeremy turns down the corridor to her office. No part of Karen's demeanor suggests she might not be serious. And yet, Jeremy finds himself asking her if she is serious when she fires him. The dead-end discussion lasts less than eight minutes. Karen has trouble excoriating his performance-since-hire. He is of so little interest to her. She says only, she expected more from a fellow alum.

He is back on the street by eleven, his arms around a shopping bag with the dartboard sticking out. He shakes off his embarrassment. This is what he was going to do, anyway. At home, there are two calls from the designers and one from Nina. Lucky she called. In the upset, he had forgotten about his mother. He calls the designers while fixing himself an omelet. He is still eating when he speed dials Nina.

She answers, "Hey, champ, how is every thing-a-ling-a-ling?"

Jeremy puts a bite in his mouth and swallows. "It's swell how nobody has to say 'hello' any more now we all have caller i.d."

"Swell? Where are you calling from, Jeremy, the fifties?"

"Don't tease. I was fired this morning."

"Oh. Sorry. That sucks. But you were planning to quit. No?" Jeremy doesn't answer because his mouth is full. "Hey, are you eating?"

He swallows again. "Yes. I am trying to remember to. Haven't been eating enough."

"Well, watch yourself, kiddo. Don't get all depleted just because you're on a roll."

"I know." He pauses. "Listen, how's Mum? I had a weird call from her this morning."

"Yeah, that's why I called you. I told her about the attack."

"Why?"

"I was there and she was being, oh, just so herself. I brought you up. How wonderful it was to see you, and about your invention, blah, blah, blah . . . She said you asked for money. Just the way she said it, pissed me off. The next thing I knew, I was telling her how we had been mugged."

"Jesus, Nina, that probably wasn't smart. How'd she take it?"

"Like she'd been hit by a truck."

"Did she say anything?"

"After she got done being quiet, she asked why we hadn't told her sooner. I bumbled through. The whole thing was dreadful. I immediately regretted it."

"When was this?"

"Last week."

"Why didn't you call then?"

"Well, I didn't see any reason to. I guess I didn't want to tell you why I'd spilled the beans. About her being cold. Then, I got a call from her sounding pretty jazzed, singing your praises."

"Yeah, that's what she was like with me."

"Do you think maybe Uncle Alan has been talking you up? Talking up the project?"

"I guess that's a possibility but she didn't say anything like that."

"Huh."

"And she jumped off quickly, that's what was really strange, and didn't pick up when I called back."

"OK. I'll check in on her and let you know."

"Thanks. It worried me."

They move on to the twins and Oscar. Jeremy gives Nina a progress report. He tells her he has a date with an old friend this evening. Nina wishes him every kind of luck.

"At a minimum, have sex."

"What would I do without you, Sis?" he drawls.

"I've no idea," she says.

Alejandro sits up in bed. He watches Jeremy in his underwear, pacing in front of the wall of sketches. Jeremy's strides make the drawings flutter.

"Come, get some sleep, Jeremy."

"I'm antsy."

"I can see that." Alejandro watches his friend. "You've got a weird energy coming off of you."

"Yeah, I know." There is a quality of agitated insistence in his voice, he can hear it himself, even when he is agreeing. "I might have to head back to New York. Something seems to be up with my mother. I talked to Nina today."

"Your mother," says Alejandro. He blows out of both nostrils with disgust. The men have been friends for years. Alejandro has heard all about Edith, the whole family saga. "You don't owe her anything."

"While that might have been true at one point, it isn't any longer. She helped me get the ball rolling."

"She funded you?"

"No. But she talked to an uncle who did."

"I see." He thinks. "What I've never been able to grasp about the whole story re: your mother . . ." Alejandro sighs. "Why didn't you just tell her you were gay?"

"I did. We both did, Nina and I, but it didn't make a difference."

Alejandro takes this in. "You know that is strange. Right?"

"I do."

"She did not care you were gay <u>and</u> it did not convince her you were not molesting your sister?"

"You got it."

"So strange."

"Well, I think she had a visceral reaction and, about the gayness, I was fifteen. I mean, I had no experience. I think she didn't believe me. Not really."

"Your dad was fine with everything?"

"He was."

"OK, indulge me here?" Jeremy nods and Alejandro rolls over onto his back, thinking. "You got a cig?" Jeremy scrounges around in his side table and finds one. Alejandro lights up and lies back again. "You ready, baby, 'cause I'm building a theory."

"Let's have it," says Jeremy, smiling widely for the first time since breakfast.

"Your father's family built an empire, right?"

"Yes."

"The wealth in some form survives to this day, but it is unmade, over and over, by a 'curse' of 'optimism.' From whom did you hear this story, your mother or your father?"

Jeremy thinks. "Both. More often from Mum, I guess."

"OK, there is this cautionary tale. Then, when you are fifteen, your mother has an outsized reaction to an incident between you and your sister. Goes all schizophrenogenic."

"Goes what?"

"Never mind. Old discredited theory of mothers who drive their healthy kids mad. Not important. Anyway, your coming out does not persuade her there was no harm."

Jeremy nods.

"Some piece is missing." Alejandro thinks.

Jeremy looks over at Alejandro on the bed, his remarkable torso resting on the pillows. He is a beautiful man. Loveable. Why has it never come to anything more than this? Dr. Somayaji floats through Jeremy's mind. He realizes the doctor's dark eyes have the shape and depth of Alejandro's.

"Eventually, she came around?"

"Never completely. She shut me out. She came to accept we were telling the truth but she never completely let me back in after that."

"Did she accuse you directly of messing around with Nina?"

"No."

"But she made you leave?"

"Yes, I was sent home early, to Dad, in New York."

"And you would go home now if she needs you?"

"I would."

Alejandro watches Jeremy who has started to pace again.

"Have you ever considered talking to anyone about this? I mean, professionally?"

"Never. How would it change anything? She is the way she is."

Alejandro does not try to persuade him. He pats the bed beside him.

"OK, I don't have the whole picture, yet, but you need to settle," says Alejandro. "You're flickering like the dust in one of your snow globes."

The next morning, Jeremy wakes to find Alejandro has slipped out. When Jeremy makes the bed, he sees Alejandro left him a note tucked under the edge of his water glass. He lifts the glass and reads the note. It skirts the edge of romantic. It's a playful thank you and a promise to call.

Jeremy goes to the kitchen to make breakfast but is immediately drawn to a list of people to contact before the day is out. He skips breakfast, gets himself coffee and begins to work his way down the list. A call comes in while he is speaking with a possible supplier. He puts his call on hold to answer. It is Nina. She tells him only their mother seems more positive than usual.

"Sunny, I would say."

"The 'fatal sunniness' was on Dad's side of the family," says Jeremy.

"Yeah, I know."

"Well, you know what this means, then?"

"Her cheerfulness isn't likely to kill her," says Nina. They agree Nina will call Edith in another few days to check in. Jeremy is relieved it does not seem to be anything dire. He turns his attention back to work and does not break until late afternoon when Alejandro calls.

"Can I entice you to lunch tomorrow?"

"I'm trying to plow through so much this week. I'm expecting the prototype."

"But you have all those extra hours since you were fired. Fill one with me. I'm pretty sure of something."

"What?"

"I'll tell you when I see you."

It is a beautiful and typically clear L.A. day when Jeremy finds himself within sight of Alejandro, outside, at their favorite vegan spot. Jeremy isn't vegan, like Alejandro, but he appreciates the chef at this place. They kiss hello and order. As the two men wait, Alejandro leans toward Jeremy. He has a special look of satisfaction in his eye. He begins with a brief review: the family means, the historical curse of failed enterprises, Jeremy's feeling trapped by this legacy, the reaction to the bathing incident, the father's acceptance, the mother's rejection, the attack, Jeremy's current project, and his mother's sudden cheerfulness. He then pivots to Jeremy's difficulties with sleep and eating. Alejandro asks a few questions and then puts his chin in his hand. He looks at Jeremy quietly for a moment.

"You are named for your father's family. This is a burden you carry. Or so you have said . . ."

Jeremy opens his mouth to qualify this, but Alejandro stops him with his hand.

"Many times. There are stories of accumulated grandeur but also of a flaw that accompanies the name. It is a mystery. One your mother participates in by repeating the story and never discussing money."

"Yes?"

"I think it's a smoke screen."

"What?"

"Your mother is fierce, right?"

"I wouldn't use that adjective but, OK, in a way."

"Like a mother bear."

"Well, no, there you're wrong. She's not protective. Remember she stranded me, for years, without her love. And she doesn't even see the twins. Or, not often. Who doesn't see their grandchildren?"

Alejandro considers this.

"Did she have a sibling?"

"Yeah, a sister who died at seventeen."

"Her sister died," says Alejandro as if he has just scored a point. "How?"

"A driver didn't stop at a light; Mum never wanted to talk about it."

"Your mom loved you when you were little?"

"Yes."

"And your sister? Was she close to her?"

"In her own way. She always approved of Nina but was never cozy with her the way she was with me. That didn't change."

"Her return to calling you 'darling' came right after you described your project? A game about naming."

"Yes."

"And her odd cheerfulness after she learned of the attack?"

"Uh huh."

"Well, it's beginning to make sense to me."

"How?"

"I don't think it was ever about incest. What was her sister's name?"

"Alma."

"Alma was seventeen when she died?"

"Yeah."

"How old was Nina that summer when you were fifteen?"

"She is fifteen months older than me."

"So in August she was . . ."

Jeremy calculates their relative birthdays. "Seventeen."

When Jeremy returns from lunch, the UPS gal, in her brown uniform, is getting back into her truck. He jogs over. She has the prototype. His hands shake slightly as he signs for the package. Once inside, he telephones Nina. He wants to tell her about Alejandro's hunch and he wants to put her on speakerphone before he opens the package. The tremor that came on by the truck has spread through his body. His limbs hum. Nina does not want to hear Alejandro's nascent theory about their mom. She is much more interested in the package. She asks Jeremy to describe the gizmo as he unwraps it. In step-by-step fashion, Jeremy talks her through the unveiling. When Jeremy lifts the large globe, with its ornate burnished handle and base, and the beetle, beautifully reproduced, with its red wing spots and a dramatic black cross on its back, he breathes in, awestruck. It is a perfect Panagaeus crux-major.

"I'm taking a picture with my phone, Neen, to send you right now," he says.

Once she has it, she is equally blown away. Jeremy makes her laugh with his story of Darwin's excitement on seeing "a sacred Panagaeus crux-major" when he already had two ground beetles in hand. Darwin popped one of these in his mouth, to free up a hand to catch the Panagaeus crux-major, and was treated to its defensive ejaculation. He swallowed the nasty stuff, and was so thrown off, he lost all three beetles in the process. Nina laughs and laughs.

"I'm gonna call Mum."

"Yeah, OK, what time is it there?"

They decide, instead, that Nina will take a cab over so she can show their mother on her phone. Jeremy feels himself light up. The siblings will not be in touch while Nina travels so Jeremy can spend the time seeing if he can work the damn thing. He places the globe on his table and admires it. Without any other function, it is already a success. He shakes it and watches the golden letters circle around the model. The beetle's legs are wrapped around a twig. The red and black wings shine metallically. With care, he gets the pincer to lower and begins to go after the letters. He collects the "a"s first and drops them into the embossed cavities along the wing. Next he gets the capital "p" and then the "g" and the "u"s. It is tricky but doable. It occurs to him anyone raised on video games will ace this. He congratulates himself on such a seductive analog plaything. He is almost done building the name when Nina calls back.

"Hey," he answers exuberantly, "in two seconds we're gonna see if this works."

"Jeremy," Nina whispers. He drops the handle. The "m" in his grasp sinks to the bottom of the glass.

"What is it, Nina?"

"It's Mum. She wouldn't let me in. Then she did. She has a parrot."

"She has a parrot?" asks Jeremy, attempting to understand the note of fear in Nina's voice.

"Yes, a huge green bird," whispers Nina. Jeremy's mind races back to the coffee table book with the parrot on its cover. Nina shrieks.

"Nina, are you all right? What's going on?"

"Jeremy, the bird doesn't seem to have a cage. Mum has it loose. It's flying around. It just missed me. It's shitting on everything."

"Put Mum on," orders Jeremy. There is some muffled noise. He can hear both their voices but he can't make out what they are saying.

"Jeremy," says his mother with authority.

"Mum, Nina says you have a bird without a cage?" Edith does not respond to his question.

"Jeremy," says Edith again, this time in that staccato but cheerful voice, "I have been thinking about your toy."

"Yes?" asks Jeremy although he doesn't mean to. He wants to get Nina back on the phone.

"There is a natural order. An ordering. Like your beetles." She says this too quickly as if each word were being pressed out of her. Jeremy feels a pit open in his stomach.

"Mum, put Nina on."

"In a second, dear." He hears his mother breathing heavily.

"Mum, put Nina on."

"It is so important to keep everything in order."

After the Red Eye has landed, Jeremy turns on his phone. There are a string of texts from Nina who seems to have gotten some Valium from a friend and has Oscar at the apartment. There is a text from when she got Edith to sleep at 3:30 a.m. A string of panda faces with dark-circled eyes, followed by exclamation points, signal Nina's relief. Jeremy catches a cab as soon as he can.

He hesitates for a breath, outside the door, on the maroon carpet. Turning to look at the pathetic plants by the window, his overnight bag in hand, he knocks. Nina almost pushes him over. When he can assure her he is really there, ready to roll up his sleeves, she lets him in. She wipes her eyes with both hands, her hair sticking out from her head as if she had been rolling downhill all night.

"I found something I want to show you," Nina whispers.

"Why are you whispering?"

"I'm terrified of when she wakes. Oh, Jeremy." Nina heaves a sigh. Her eyes fill. "We have to take her to the hospital once she's up. She needs something stronger than what we've got and expert eyes on her."

"Did she ever calm down?"

"For very brief snatches. The Valium finally knocked her out. We had to give her a ton. Mostly, she was talking a blue streak as if it were absolutely urgent to communicate everything in her mind. A lot of nonsense about the 'natural order' and keeping things in place. Also about us, you and me, and our not coming to harm from the dangers of love. Nutty stuff."

Jeremy flashes to Alejandro's theory.

"Oh, and her plan to move to the Amazon with Philippe."

"The parrot?"

Nina nods and hands Jeremy an album, from a messy stack of records on the sideboard.

"Philippe Jaroussky," Jeremy reads to himself.

"But, to tell you the truth, the bird sounds more like a sailor than a French countertenor."

"Poor Mum."

"Yeah, just you wait. She is a force to be reckoned with. I've never seen her so domineering. She wanted to buy a ticket last night. Really hard to get her to let that go. And then there is this thing . . . I'm gonna go find it for you."

In the early morning light, the apartment does not look that different. Jeremy had spent the night, shifting in his narrow seat aboard the plane, imagining a madhouse. Instead there is sensible Oscar, bent over the coffee table in rubber gloves, cleaning. On another pass, Jeremy can see there are white globs and streaks on many surfaces. The bird, however, is nowhere in evidence.

"We got him caged sometime after midnight." Oscar answers Jeremy's searching look. "Really massive bird. Nuts about your mum. A lot of salty language, though she doesn't seem to mind."

"Hey, get over here," says Jeremy.

Oscar wiggles his rubber gloves comically as he moves in for a bear hug. As they separate, Nina appears with a box. She sets it down by the couch.

"This is going to bloody blow your mind," says Oscar.

Nina just looks up at Jeremy with her own red-rimmed eyes. Jeremy sits next to her.

His agitation rises. Fear reaches out from a shadowy place within what he thinks he knows and grips him. Nina hands him a picture of two girls, the same height, with crowns of curls. They are maybe ten or eleven and identical.

"Wait, that's Mum?" Jeremy looks at Nina stunned. "Edith and Alma were twins?"

Nina nods.

"Why didn't she ever tell us?"

Nina doesn't answer him until after she has shown him the whole treasure trove of the girls, dressed alike at every stage, from infancy to early adolescence. Nina's face clouds. "There are no pictures of Alma, I assume its Alma, after thirteen or so. There are pictures only of Mum."

"But I thought Alma died at seventeen?"

"She did," says Nina. "But look . . ." Nina hands him a newspaper clipping. It is an obituary on faded newsprint. The fragment is creased from being handled and refolded, over and over. It is hard to make out but Jeremy reads:

> Alma Alice Stokes, June 6th, 1952 – November
> 25th, 1969, beloved daughter of Esther and
> Nathan Stokes and sister of Edith Anne Stokes.
> May she rest in Peace. Donations can be made to
> The Steppes Newelpost Home, 110 Cedar Drive,
> Shaker Heights, Ohio or Angel of Mercy Church,
> 59 Main Street, Bedford, Ohio.

"There is no mention of a service," says Jeremy.

"Or a car accident. And Jeremy?"

"Hm?"

"The 'Home'?"

Jeremy looks his question.

"No longer in operation but it was . . ."

"A mental institution?" asks Jeremy.

In a darkened booth midtown Jeremy waits. He rises as an elegant gentleman joins him.

"I can't thank you enough for helping us find the right team," says Jeremy. Dr. Somayaji smiles at him as he folds himself into the booth.

"Happy to," he says.

Lagoon

The scrubbed linoleum showed patches of a featureless sublayer. Big Jim, his metal chair rocked against the wall, was leaning forward, on the edge of the seat, feet planted on the floor, head in hands, awash in regret. His white handlebar mustache seemed to drag his features toward his boots. The boots with the extra wide toe box. Drawn in tight to his chin, his mustache was anchored by the muscles of a mouth that, for the last hour, had been locked in a grimace. He was not in physical pain. He had sequestered himself in the hallway, outside the waiting room of the local hospital, to avoid seeing anyone he knew. He was an accessory to the insult. Actually, it was worse than that.

Lacey came through the door and looked the other way before spotting him behind the door. "What are you doing out here?" she asked. As soon as Big Jim saw her features, he was run through with gratitude.

"It was the shirt. I thought he was a turkey," Big Jim pleaded.

Lacey looked at the gouty wreck in front of her.

"He is," she said.

Two days earlier, Lacey had gotten a call from Big Jim. She was finishing up with an aggrieved taxpayer who wanted to know the process for an abatement. She explained to Ned Hickey (whom she saw many times a week) that the form could be downloaded from the town website or picked up directly from her. She reminded him he only had ten days. The filing needed to be within thirty days of the date the tax bills were mailed. Intermittently, Lacey watched her dad blinking on the other line. Eventually, she picked him back up. Big Jim was in a terrible state.

"You been drinking beer?" she began, when she heard how hard it was for him to stand.

"It doesn't matter. It's uric acid that builds up."

"I know," said Lacey, "but beer makes it worse."

"Your putting me on hold makes it worse."

"OK. What is it you need?"

This was how, before her morning was even properly started, she'd left affairs in Minnow Lassiter's hands and gone to collect her dad. He needed to go into the center, to pick up his prescription glasses. He could not drive his truck. Since the flare started, he said, the slightest pressure on his toe was excruciating. She argued with him about calling his doctor.

"Why don't you move back into the house?" asked Big Jim. Lacey felt a tug in her chest cavity like wallpaper being pried loose from a wall. It made her feel her next breath too strongly.

"I'm happy where I am." She pulled into the plaza parking lot and parked. It turned out the glasses were going to take another couple of days.

"That's nuts," said Big Jim when Lacey got back in the truck. "I won't have them 'till Monday."

"Don't you have a backup pair?"

"Ned sat on them."

This was the same Ned. Ned Hickey. "Listen, I need to pick up some salt hay for Maureen. I'll drop you home after Agway."

"I want to head right back."

"You'll have to make do. I'll be fast."

Ned Hickey and Charlie were waiting when they pulled in.

"Don't any of you ever work?" Lacey asked her dad, eyeing the guys on the porch through the truck's windshield.

"Watch yourself."

"Seriously, though."

"Well, I'm laid up and the guys probably swung by on their way to fix Rot Lane culvert."

"Just as long as they didn't bring beer."

"It's eleven in the morning, puffball."

"Don't call me that."

"Why not, sugar pie?"

Lacey parked the truck and helped her dad to the house. Jim told the guys he would be back on the job in a couple of days. Lacey doubted this was true. Charlie began praising West Hyack's decision to buy a new grader. He felt skeptical their town would vote the plow. Soon, the three men were caught up in a relative analysis of equipment and the politics of folks who'd moved to town from away.

Lacey excused herself to deliver the hay.

Along Cagney Hill, you see the valley of the Ponotuck and Blood Rivers as it stretches all the way into Connecticut. There are peaceable stories of European settlers encountering the family groups that held the region. Before that, there are origin stories. Big Jim's hunting cabin was not far from this look out, up a steep dirt way. Close to the cabin, the drive was lined with painted rocks. You needed a serious vehicle to get in there. The cabin was basically one room with a porch hanging off the front. Black streaks of mold marked the siding, the discoloration running unevenly up the face. Lacey checked its ugliness often but felt good about the cabin's interior where the action took place.

Although there was a wood-burning stove, the cabin had to be wrapped in plastic during the winter. It was a stretch to call it as a three-season building. Big Jim had built it for deer and bear. Facing the cabin, to the left, a separate shed held firewood and tools. Since Lacey moved in three years ago, she used the shed to spray-paint rocks blue.

The morning of the event, sideways in the bed, Lacey scanned the bookshelf and misread a spine from bottom to top, jumbling the letters into "snot." Some title, she thought while the letters rearranged themselves, in their real order, still backwards. She saw she'd left out the "k." The cover was faded. It was, right side up, a book about knots.

Lacey squinted at her relic of a bedside clock. The superannuated face, bland and forthright despite winters without heat, continued to tick as if it knew nothing about time's passage or its currency. In this lazy cataloging, Lacey rolled over and singled out a knothole in the floor. Morning light filtered back to her bed from the dirty front windows and caught on the rough edge in the whorl.

Big Jim had had to teach Lacey to tie a bowline every summer— one of four essential boating knots. Lacey can't remember the others. The refrain, and its frustrated repetition, came back. Up through the rabbit hole, 'round the tree; down through the rabbit hole and off goes he. It can be tied with one hand—useful if you're holding a boat. It is easy to untie even after bearing a load (the boat). Lacey wonders if the difficulty she had holding onto this skill was her father's certainty it was important or his conviction it was easy? Every single summer. Well, it didn't matter now.

Lacey turned on her back and drew her knees up to her chest. She drew in a long slow breath. She felt a flutter as she heard the tread on her porch. How had she missed the sound of James Sheedy's Jeep? A light rap and the squeak of the cabin door opening followed the footfall.

"Hey, what are you doing not up? It's 9:00."

"It's Saturday."

"But we're going fishing."

"The fish don't know that."

James rolled his eyes.

"What?" said Lacey, taking in this other Jim. "The whole point of fishing is fish-head."

"Fish-head?"

"Getting yours as empty as a Punky's."

"Really?" said James. He looked at Lacey lolling on the bed, her shirt rucked up above her generous middle, her pale sand thong. He felt the stir too but there would be time for that later.

"How was the drive up?"

"Not bad. I came in last night," said James.

"What time did you get off the set?"

"Late."

James made his way across the clothing-strewn floor and into Lacey's arms. He was a great kisser. She had teased him he could go pro. Wrapping herself around him, Lacey felt the smooth fibers of his shirt. When she came up for air she said, "That's one heck of a city flannel you've got going on there." The shirt was various greens woven with burnt sienna lines.

"You like it?"

"I do," she said.

"Well, that's lucky."

.   .   .

Once outside, Lacey asked, "And why is it lucky?" They were standing beside the Jeep. She ran her hand up his arm. James did not answer her. Instead he reached in through the open window and brought out a package. Lacey ducked her head, touched.

Wearing her new shirt, Lacey was careful taking lunch from the orange Jeep. She didn't want to snag the fabric. It was a two-mile hike to the pond. Ridiculous to wear this luxury into the brush, she thought. She would stow it as soon as she was warm. The morning was cool, but the day would soon heat up. She let her eye glide over the edge of her sleeve to James's. It was like a contract, these matching shirts; the novelty of his claim prevented her protesting the gift's misuse.

The pond wasn't technically on Big Jim's property, but the access road was the dirt way to the cabin. It went past the cabin, in about a mile. The only other route was over land. The parcel belonged to a family of dairy farmers who had held hundreds and hundreds of acres spread over the valley. In memory, many of the farms had disappeared as subsidies favored bigger dairy and the men migrated to other work. When Big Jim was a kid, the owner's local standing had inspired fear, although the patriarch often carried candy in his tractor on days when Big Jim went to help with the fencing.

As Lacey and James neared the end of their climb, they were still in deep woods. Only at the water's edge could you see where beavers had cleared a far shore. Behind this grassy beach, the hillside rose up steeply to a ridgeline. Up there, a ledge looked down on the water's surface as it caught moving clouds over an area large enough to qualify as a small lake.

The water body was marked on maps as Squaw Pond, but Big Jim and Lacey had christened it "the lagoon" when she was fourteen, her mom had passed, and they'd launched the flat bottomed skiff Big Jim named after his departed wife. Her loss had gutted both of them. Lacey and Big Jim had to push the skiff through muddy reeds, alive with frogs, to get to open water. When the boat was free, Big Jim, with tears running down his craggy face, looked down at his skinny girl, watching the skiff with her mother's name across the stern, dry-eyed. Jim had wondered if, along with being gutted, Lacey had also been cauterized. Ned and Charlie had helped with the portage from the access road. They had been sworn to secrecy. Even with three strong men, it had been a feat to haul it up there. Like Big Jim's lost mate, the Patty-Anne was built solid.

Lacey led James to the place where the skiff was tied. She'd long since shucked her shirt and safely packed it. It was mid-morning but the peepers were acting like it was dawn.

"Put your shoes in the boat so we can push her out," said Lacey.

James looked at the grassy shoreline. There were ripples among the grasses.

"Is there anything up in the water?"

Lacey turned toward James with her hands on her hips. "Fish, we hope," she said.

"Yeah, I know, but . . ."

"What you spooked by?"

"Leeches?"

Tossing her sneakers in the skiff, Lacey barked a laugh that echoed from the opposite shore and hung in the air. Along the south side of the lagoon, at intervals, no trespassing signs still hung on boards gone grey with age. The owner long ago ineffectually cast his net, as James had, over a wilderness.

· · ·

They struck out for the far side because the fish were best close to the beaver-cleared shore. About halfway, they decided to stop and drift. The heat of the day enclosed them in an envelope. The fish weren't biting. Lacey glanced at James in the stern, sideways on his seat, reeling in his cast. They were riding low in the smooth water, having brought along a lot of gear. James liked to be prepared. He turned back a slow and glassy look. She could see his head was emptying. In his piscine gaze, Lacey felt herself like a school of sunfish performing a liquid ballet in the shallows. So she secured her rod along the gunwale and clambered back to him. The boat rocked. James came to attention as her hand met his damp pant cuff.

The seats, and a raised seam running the length of the hull, complicated the undertaking. James peeled off his shirt and threw it casually in the stern. High above Lacey, and dimly focused on the satin sun reflecting off near water, James's weigh shifted too far to the left. The pair failed to register the list except as part of what they were up to. Only when the grip of the moment played out did the water leaking over the side make Lacey sit upright and shout at James to bring his weight to center. The beamy skiff, cumbersome and heavy, was not easy to capsize but taking water could sink it like a stone. James moved quickly but instead of stabilizing them, the violent correction set the boat rocking and more water flowed in. They were suddenly riding dangerously close to the water. Lacey ordered James to bail but he could not find the bailer among the bobbing gear. They had to change places for Lacey to fish through the bilge water and find it.

They were in a precarious position. Their wet gear weighted the skiff. Even their lunch, supposedly protected in a soft cooler, was soggy.

"We need to pack it in," said Lacey.

"Aw, shoot."

"Sorry, but the skiff's too heavy."

James raised a playful eyebrow at Lacey. "But we didn't catch anything," he said as petulantly as a six year old. She felt a sensation like an internal scraping against her perineum. Having never been pregnant, she did not know this feeling mimicked the grind of an infant's head against the pelvic floor. Lacey directed James to row as she bailed.

"Depends on what you were angling for," said Lacey. She paused and looked at his large head.

"At least, that's lookin' good 'n empty," she said, circling her finger at his noggin.

"Baby, you emptied my whole being."

"Oh yeah. Me and the fish."

"That's what I'm talkin' 'bout," said James.

She knew he thought he'd landed in some kind of crazy paradise. She could not fathom where he lived most of the time— the whole urban deal. Looking at his blemish-less face, without freckles like her own, Lacey thought of all the excess: people, noise, chichi food, traffic, tall buildings, car alarms. What kind of person adds to this a job scheduling high-speed chases, cast and crew, explosions? Although she had only had small town tax experience, she had opinions. Neither the real shit, or the make-believe kind, seemed worth their valuation.

Taking the oars from him, she turned the skiff expertly and pulled toward the closest shore. James asked if he could cast as they rowed. She told him, as long as they were within easy swim of shore, she could bring them along the bank and give him some good water. When Lacey reached the right distance from the bank, he cast out. He drew the line back in, watching the parting wake along the thread. She watched his arms in the light, city-white, russet haired, and muscled as a statue's.

It was not long before he had a bend in the line. With Lacey's coaching, he brought it in until, after a last fighting tug, the fish broke water—a small river trout. It gleamed, flipping on the hook. Again, with Lacey's help, James maneuvered the trout to the side of the boat where Lacey, having shipped the oars, had a net ready. James looked at its green-gold speckled back and the rosy strip along its side. He felt a shiver of responsibility for its life but his heart was pumping with the satisfaction of capture.

"That's gonna make a tasty morsel," said Lacey.

Watching her resume the oars, James thought back to the church basement where he had first seen one of her constructions. Then, she wasn't painting rocks blue. When they first met, last spring, at the opening of a local show, hers had been the watery paintings of foraged plants—ramps, nettles, morels—framed in galvanized steel culvert piping. They were curious "outsider" art. Clearly, she knew a thing or two. But when he approached her, he could not get past the surface. She deflected all his questions, leaving him, between this resistance and her pliant body, hot with curiosity.

Now that he had made a catch, she directed the skiff to a sandy patch between water lilies. The trout was still flopping in the bottom of the boat.

"Shouldn't we hit its head or something?" asked James.

"Naw. It will stop soon. I need you to jump in and haul us up."

Gingerly, but gamely, James put his foot over the side. Then, he splashed in up to his knees and made Lacey laugh by rapidly describing the way the bottom felt.

"Slimy, slimy, slimy, sandy, ack, ouch, pebbles."

"Just haul us up, sailor," Lacey laughed.

On his way past, James reached deep and yanked a water-lily up by its root. He presented the flower, drooping from the long slippery stem.

Once the skiff was up and the wet gear unpacked, they shook off what they could, wringing out whatever was wring-able. James delicately draped his shirt over a bush just behind them, in a clearing, in full sun. When he returned, they flipped the Patty-Anne on her side and tipped her far enough to let the remaining water drain. James noticed Lacey assumed as much of the weigh as she could when they let her rock back toward them and down into the sandy mud. She secured the skiff to a birch whose new leaves were so different from her (whose name described them). Lacey and James were not far from the actual beach. They decided to pack up their lunch and strike out for it with the aim to either take their picnic there or hike up to the ledge. James changed into a t-shirt of some elite material.

"That's not cotton is it?" Lacey asked, eyeing it skeptically.

"Cotton kills," he answered, flashing his white teeth.

For such a slicker, he had certain skills even in the woods. It took them only twenty-five minutes to make the beach. They stripped off their clothes and dove in. The water was clear by the beach and fresh-water soft. James took Lacey's body in his arms and told her she weighed nothing. He swung her, floating, across the surface of the water in an arc from his body. Lacey allowed herself to go slack. She watched the two clouds above rotate from one side of her field of vision to the other, back and forth. There was nothing else above and only the light touch of his arms below.

"Let's climb up to the ledge."

"If you want. But the view from here is already spectacular," James crooned. He bent forward so his lips brushed her nipple. Lacey jackknifed out of his arms and swam away. She stood at a distance. He hadn't moved. His arms were akimbo, half hidden below the water. He smiled at her and, putting his hands around his mouth, as if she were a football field away, he gave an exaggerated shouted.

"You are a strong swimmer, Lacey." Lacey smiled back and jerked her head toward shore, indicating they both should wade in. She unpacked the trout and proceeded to clean it.

"Make yourself useful and gather some firewood."

"I can't. Watching you do that naked has me transfixed."

"Then, throw me my shirt, 'cause I'm starving."

He shook his head, so she got up and retrieved it herself. Once she was semi-covered, James reluctantly did as he was told. He scavenged wood and made a passable campfire inside a ring of rocks. Lacey got out the cook kit and waterproof matches.

"Can you tell me about your stones?" James tried.

"Not while I'm cooking over this thing."

"Just give me a hint."

She gestured toward the sky, taking it in with a wide sweep of her hand.

The fish was delicious. Only when they were fed did Lacey open herself a second time to him on the sand.

The view from the ledge was wide and deep. It contained the valley to Connecticut and beyond, to more distant hills, within a rolling landscape. A haze hung blue-gray over the horizon. From the outcropping, the lagoon lay still and reflective below. It was almost a perfect circle, blue as one of Lacey's stones.

Except for the skiff, breaking the edge, heading out on its own, toward the lake's center.

"Shit," cried Lacey.

"Oh, fuuuck," echoed James.

It took them forty minutes of scrambling to get back down and to the spot where the boat had launched herself. It was now seventy yards offshore. One more time, Lacey stripped and waded into the water.

"You stay here."

"Why?" asked James.

"In case I need reinforcements."

Without waiting for his answer she dove. Breaking the surface, she began powerful slow strokes out toward the skiff. Because the day was windless, the boat was barely moving. It almost seemed at anchor. Lacey reached it without too much effort but it was a bitch to pull herself up and over. A loose nail caught her side as she dragged herself over the gunwale. It tore a small notch that bled down her stomach. Like Jesus, she thought.

Lacey was already at the oars when she heard the shot and a sound of something falling.

"James!"

There was no reply. Lacey pulled on the oars with everything she had, which caused them to jump the oarlocks. This cost her time. While she had been blind to the necessity of knots, she had bothered, as a kid, to learn the techniques of rowing. She lifted the oars back into place and concentrated on pulling evenly, her hands gliding purposefully, the left just below the right. Her heart was racing but she calmed her breath and did not shout again.

Finally near to shore, Lacey heard movement on land. Hopeful and raging, she called out again over her shoulder.

"James."

With a final strong pull she slid in across the water lilies, shipping her oars as the boat slipped in. She stood, turned, and climbed over the side. Racing, she grabbed up the dripping painter from below the water and hauled the Patty Anne up as best she could, laid the line in a sandy depression, and dropped a large stone over it. This took practically no time. As she was grunting and moving, she could hear a thrashing sound in the near-by brush. This was how she came upon Big Jim crouched down with his shotgun under one arm and his other hand outstretched and touching James's head.

"What did you do?" shouted Lacey.

The old man recoiled. Before he could offer an explanation, she shoved him aside to minister to James. He was bare-chested but had the flannel part way up one sleeve. Why? Maybe he was dressing when the bullet clipped him. Maybe he had changed, and then reconsidered, and was caught undressing to swim out and join her. Whatever it was, his exposed shoulder allowed her to see instantly he had only been winged. The wound did not look too bad. She slipped the fancy shirt back off his arm and staunched the wound with it. The soft material was a perfect surgical sponge. She looked at his ashen face. He was too unfocused for the grazed shoulder to be the whole explanation. His eyes were open but unseeing. He had yet to speak. Then, she saw the puddle of purple-red blood in the grass behind his ear. When he went down, his head must have hit a rock.

She did not ask her dad what he was doing all the way up here, with his gouty foot, at the side of the lagoon, with a shotgun. Instead she enlisted him.

"Help me get him sitting up."

Big Jim moved in wordlessly to do this but Lacey threw out a hand at the last minute.

"James, can you hear me?"

He blinked up at her as if he were in a cave but crawling out. There was a delay. Then, he nodded.

"We're gonna get you sitting to see what's what. Do you think your neck is OK?"

Again, James didn't answer but slowly turned his head back and forth a little. Enough, Lacey thought. On its way past, his look reached her. It seemed to repeat, you emptied me completely.

"Get him under his back on the side you didn't shoot him," snarled Lacey at her dad.

"OK, sugar pie," said Big Jim in a hangdog voice. "I'm sorry."

"Save it," said Lacey.

A nurse touched Lacey on the back, through the light flannel, as Lacey hung out the door speaking to Big Jim. Lacey turned, thinking she would make James a gift of one of her rocks, maybe the cerulean one.

"You can both come in now," the nurse said. They found James sitting up in bed, bandaged over his shoulder, across his chest, and around his head. His reddish hair flopped over the bandage in a way Lacey found lovely.

"How's the head?" asked Lacey.

"Empty as a Punky's," said James.

"Atta boy," said Lacey.

Law of Attraction Fundamentals

A disheveled man with a fifth of Jack in a paper bag squinted at the screen of his neighbor's phone. He could not hear the sound as it traveled up the white cords into the ears of a creature on the seat beside him. But he could read the words: *Two Critical Mistakes that Cause Most Manifestation Projects to Fail.* These hovered at the bottom of the image, over a talking head, against a tropical waterfall. The presenter's lips flapped silently. Behind his head an out-of-focus Toucan sailed by. The words at the bottom of the screen shifted. The crusty reader's focus wasn't perfect. He made out, "*Guarantee Your Success,*" and looked away. He turned his attention to his own shoe. He tipped further forward, examining the side where the cloth was about to give, as if this weakness contained the answer, and, without malice or restraint, farted.

Penelope Wendall, riveted by the instructional video, was taken up short by the sudden sulfurous stink. Pressing the pause arrow, she rose, collected her wheeled bag, and scouted for a better perch. She took in the human swirl around her. Women of every shape spilled from tube tops. They were the drosophilae of this particular hot June experiment. Some slapped by in loose slides. Some chatted among themselves, their earlobes distended by heavy bangles. Some were in charge of children. A young man with a bleached faux-hawk, his ears bristling with piercings, crouched over his seat, eyes closed, so intent on the beat from his device he appeared to be davvening. Not that Penelope made this association. She was busy taking in his kilt. Who wears a kilt in this weather?

Penelope rarely had to endure the squalor of a city bus terminal. Back when she drove more often to Iowa she had to stop wherever was available. Then, she'd once seen a truck driver menacing a similarly reedy kid. She did not know the imagined crime. As she headed to the ladies room, she overheard the driver threatening to shove something up "where the sun don't shine." Now, the memory intensified her discomfort in the small chilled station in Springfield. Everything private about her pinched shut in protest.

"For crying out loud," she muttered to herself.

Twenty more minutes to wait. Penelope took stock. She breathed in slowly through her nose and let her eyelids close, fighting for acceptance of the people snapping gum around her. After twenty seconds, she abandoned the project, opened her eyes and considered waiting outside, despite the fact that in the last hour the temperature had climbed to ninety degrees. She veered toward the vendor at the side of the station.

She purchased an ice tea, worried about the sorry looking fruit and left the stand. She would not be in Boston until 5:45. The trick on the bus was to sit at the very front so the only view was the driver behind the wheel and the unfurling highway ahead as it revealed itself and then disappeared under the bus. She would pretend the ride was for her alone, removing any trace of the bus stop. She would return to the tropical scene and commit the steps to memory. She would manifest happiness. Penelope turned back into the shop and purchased a bag of pretzels.

.   .   .

Two hours and thirty-five minutes later, she descended the steps of the bus and was met by radiant heat from the pavement. But if the ground was infernally hot, the air was decidedly cooler. A breeze had picked up. She would take this as a good omen.

She accepted her case from the driver and rolled it into the station. South Station, busy at rush hour, was still airy compared to the bus terminal. Penelope located the subway stairs. She remembered to experience gratitude for Chris and her excellent instructions. However, the turnstile immediately challenged her good will. Penelope could not maneuver her bulky bag through; the wheels caught on the edge of the narrow channel, the bag was too heavy to lift. Always slight, despite yoga, at forty-six her bookishness held sway over her muscle tone. The crowd streamed around her, pressing on her and bringing a hint of bile into her mouth. Just when she was on the brink of taking back her expansive mantra, a tall man in a suit reached for her bag and, without a word, swung it over, and waited for her to come through to collect it. Penelope pushed through the gate, thanking him in a tumble of words drowned out by the sound of the bustle. The young man lifted two fingers, touched his forehead in salute, and was off with the crowd to make the train. Penelope stood still. For a breath, she closed her eyes again and drew in the subway air. She blinked her eyes open and proceeded down to the platform. She would wait for the next train. No doubt it would be less full.

In this state, she watched as the doors closed over the passengers. They opened and shut several times, packing the commuters in. She saw her man-from-the-turnstile pressed between others like a junkyard car being compacted. Funny if you weren't in the compartment. Finally, the train began to roll. Penelope was practically alone with her bag as the train pulled out of the station. She gave a sigh of relief. But no sooner had the darkness of the tunnel swallowed the departing train than the platform was full again. With a jolt, Penelope realized she would have to get on a crowded car. Penelope was not claustrophobic, she didn't think. Still, she began cursing Chris under her voice.

The next train was in the station before panic entirely overwhelmed her. Penelope wedged herself aboard, suitcase first. Her fellow travelers surged around her luggage like surf around stone. If delayed, what would she find? The sun down? Chris no longer waiting? Once the shifting stopped (as she had witnessed from the platform) the masses congealed into a block with room only for stray appendages—a dangling bag here, an arm overhead there. Penelope toughened herself. There was yet another wave as the last few stuffed themselves aboard and the doors began their packing motion.

In the darkness of the first tunnel, Penelope felt she'd crossed into the underworld.

At 7:10, Chris Townsend, a professionally patient person, was beginning to grow impatient. She worked with youths in recovery. For her, waiting for the good thing to happen was a daily activity. She did the count backwards again. The next train, or the one after, must disgorge her cousin. Chris had taken the step of shipping off Talia, her thirteen-year-old monster-daughter, for the week so she could focus on Penelope.

The escalator to the surface uploaded another batch of commuters. They fanned out across the pavement into the evening. Standing close to the exit, Chris was bathed in the aura of the returning workforce. The collective effect of perfumes, so bright and promising in the morning, reemerged into the steamy evening an olfactory ghost of expectations. Then, finally, Penelope's ashy bob appeared from the depths. Her eyes, always close to the surface of her face, were bulging.

"Penelope, Penelope," Chris cried and waved her arms. "You survived," she called, rushing to embrace her. To Penelope, after the horrors of transit, Chris's blond features were more welcome than a buttered muffin.

"Praise the goddess," Penelope whispered, her knuckles still in a death grip around the handle of her bag. She kissed Chris's cheek.

"I hope it wasn't too awful for you."

"No. Well. I'm not used to the crowds."

"But you found your way all right?"

"Easily navigated," said Penelope, although she hadn't been able to see out the windows to check the names of the stations. She could not read them inside the car either. She doubted the firm object pressed into her sacrum, after Park Street, was merely the handle of an umbrella. When the train came above ground at the Charles Street stop, she had wondered madly if she was already there. When it rattled back underground, her heart, she was sure, briefly stopped. There had been stretches of many seconds when Penelope was not sure she could breathe. It had felt like drowning.

"The car is just over here," said Chris, leading Penelope to a red Dodge. Much to her surprise, as Penelope settled into its seat, fear and that awful clenching, left her with the suddenness of air from a burst balloon.

And here was the curious thing, thought Penelope, as the leafy Cambridge streets rolled by. Because of the regional success of a radio show she appeared on, she had more than a thousand virtual friends. With these, for all her self-imposed strictures and reticence, once a heart became an option, she repeatedly chose it. She apparently didn't simply "like" things. A steady stream of love issued from her in showers of clicks across the entire field of her acquaintance.

"Penelope looked out for me at summer camp," explained Chris to Matt. "I was six, away from home for the first time, and unpopular." Matt looked at his solid, pretty wife.

"I can't imagine you were ever unpopular."

"I was, though. I was shy."

"You? Shy? I can't imagine that either."

Matt would have liked a Corvette Stingray but his disappointment evaporated as soon as he rolled the red Dodge Charger off the lot. Matt had give. He had leeway. He was loyal. It showed not just in his marriage but in the way he held fast to his male friends from Hardy Elementary. And, as much as he knew Talia drove her mom crazy, Matt adored his garrulous teen. In child rearing, as in many things, he took the long view. Chris reached across the table and poured this husband another glass.

Chris was fond of saying, whenever his mix of friends were together, it only made sense if you imagined them as a room of boys all grown up. From this group, Chris had two in mind for her cousin: a divorced math teacher and a journalist who had never married.

"You guys aren't really cousins are you?" Matt asked, having not held onto the facts. "How were you at camp together? Aren't you, like, ten years apart?"

"Our moms were first cousins," said Penelope.

"Does that make you cousins?"

"It makes us second cousins."

"Penelope was a counselor at our camp," explained Chris.

Matt added this to what he knew of Penelope's life. Her fiancé, Leo, a teacher and a practiced outdoorsman, vanished into thin air twenty years ago, when Penelope was twenty-six. He'd been on the Appalachian Trail. Speculation was he'd attempted a solo climb and fallen into an inaccessible ravine. After his presumed death, Penelope, a teacher too, could no longer stand in front of a classroom of eager faces. She left teaching, borrowed heavily, and opened a bookstore. Through luck and grit the shop had done well.

A ferocious, if eccentric, reader, she stocked the requisite best sellers but specialized in books on early twentieth century mystics and the twenty-first century fads they spawned. If you wanted to know about the astral life of trees or the energetic benefits of peat, her store was the source. If you wanted to know about subtle bodies or the finer points of reincarnation, her store was the source. In and of itself, this was not so unusual. But, located in the five-college area, she also carried the current brainy stuff too—titles on gender and politics on the left.

The family praised her for having come through with resilience. Then, about ten years into the enterprise, Penelope stopped going to book fairs. She began making her buying decisions online, using an assistant's fieldwork as back up. Although she continued the radio book-gig, she called in to the station. She strayed from her home less and less often.

Innocent of Matt's review, seated at a table on their porch, Penelope appreciated a lucky alignment of the buildings that made it possible from this second story to see through two adjoining backyards and over buildings that sloped downhill to a view of the setting sun. It had not, as Penelope feared, gone down completely before her arrival. She enjoyed a last scarlet hurrah across the Western sky. The conversation wandered. From the garden below, Penelope caught the smell of roses.

Matt and Chris occupied the upper floors of a large clapboard building they owned in Somerville, just over the Cambridge line. They began by renting the ground floor to an older couple, both professors emeritus, to offset their mortgage. Then, three years into ownership, Chris and Matt watched out for Gustav in the aftermath of his wife's death, following a routine surgery, and through the lawsuit he brought against the hospital.

Gustav Fischer kept a tidy border along the fence that separated his yard from the house to their left. It had colorful perennials that cycled through the season in a play of textures. He also kept a bed devoted to roses at the foot of the yard. Since it was late June, these were blooming. Penelope didn't know this, but the flower whose fragrance reached her was a Secret Rose. It grew upright with large creamy flowers, rimmed with pink. Gustav's solace.

Under the influence of the wine, Penelope had begun to open up about her travels. She even described the horrible event with the bum at the bus stop and her random thoughts. She had both Matt and Chris in stitches.

"What is a manifestation project?" asked Matt, snorting.

"It is complicated to explain. I'll tell you another time if you're still interested. Basically, you attract to yourself whatever you wish for."

"How is that different from wishful thinking?"

"Why did you say it went without a hitch?" laughed Chris over Matt. She was still dabbing at her eyes.

"Oh, I don't know. I was frozen by the assault of it all. It is different," she said, addressing Matt, "because it works."

"It works?"

"It can."

"By wishing for things?"

"No. By attracting them."

"Huh. Here, let me top that off." Penelope smiled up at him but put two fingers across the top of her glass.

"This is another thing I'm not used to. I would be seeing double." Matt raised the bottle from her glass and steered it smoothly to his.

"You are a very cheap date," he said, smiling. "Maybe you can manifest a higher tolerance level so as not to be taken advantage of while here."

"I didn't know that was a risk." Chris cleared her throat and eyed Matt while tipping her glass toward him for a refill.

"When you are forced to live alone, you learn quickly what to avoid," Penelope continued, oblivious of her hosts' silent exchange. There was a brief awkward pause. Although from their perspective the whole point of her visit was to set her up, they wished she wouldn't refer to Leo. The mystery of his body never having been recovered made them uncomfortable. The lack of closure. As if, somehow, Penelope could have arranged it differently. They felt strongly nobody was forcing her to sustain her isolation. They believed she should have been over Leo decades ago—within six months of his disappearance, a year tops. Everyone had thought she was, but then she wasn't.

The screen door opened and shut. They heard rummaging on the terrace below. In the gloom of the early evening, Gustav Fischer's form moved out into his yard and adjusted a hose.

"Ahoy," called Matt.

Gustav turned and looked up. He waved.

"You want to come up for a glass?" Matt raised the wine bottle that was still in his hand and swung it back and forth. It was unlikely Gustav could see this from his vantage point but he called back cheerfully.

"I am just watering my roses."

"Come up," shouted Chris. Gustav stood still at the bottom of the yard.

"All right. Just for one glass," he called back. Penelope caught his German accent. For whatever reason, she found this foreign note particularly agreeable in the dusk. Below, Gustav's shadowy figure disappeared. A sprinkler went on. Penelope watched the sputtering jets become an open fan, dimly visible, arching over the flowers.

There was a knock on the hall stairs.

"Com'on in," bellowed Matt.

A courtly, professorial man, seventies, with a shock of white hair and a manner both inquisitive and reserved came through onto the deck.

"Penelope, this is our neighbor, Gustav Fischer. Gustav, this is Chris's cousin, Penelope. Second cousin. She's in for the week."

"Nice to meet you," said Gustav extending his hand.

"I caught a little of your garden before the light faded," said Penelope. "Exquisite." She smiled graciously and clasped his hand. Gustav bowed but was prevented from responding by Matt's engaging him over the choice of red or white.

"Whatever everybody is having. Where are you 'in' from?" Gustav asked her.

"I live near Amherst."

"She has a bookstore there," added Chris.

"Is that so? A fantastic location for books." He looked at her as if reading her.

"Yes, it is. My store is in Northampton."

"Even better," said Gustav.

When Penelope retired to the third floor, she found the guest room faced west. It had a terrace above the second floor's screened porch. A simple balustrade of turned wood enclosed the terrace. It was muted red and peeling. Otherwise, the deck was open to the night sky, now full of stars. The room had a narrow double bed, late nineteenth century with pineapple finials. Chris's taste (surprising for a jock) skewed toward the floral. But, despite the pillows and flounce, Penelope admired the room. She opened the door to the small half bath and took pleasure in an illustration of snakes hung above the toilet. Delicate Roman numerals, in black italic, identified each type. Obviously it had once been a bookplate. The thin red circlet around a grey snake's neck delighted her. She took off her clothes and showered. The towel was coarse as if it had been air-dried which reminded her of home.

Before changing for bed, Penelope stood naked by the open door to the terrace. Since the lights in her room were off, she was confident she was invisible from outside. The night was caressing in a way the cooler country nights, even in summer, rarely were. She needed no mirror to know she was still youthful in her skin. She reached her hands up and ran them through her short hair from the nape upwards. She turned back into the room and seated herself on an upholstered stool at the foot of the bedstead. Years of practice allowed her to move into and hold a full lotus. With her hands on her knees she cleared a space in her mind. She allowed an image of Leo to come to her. Not Leo when she last saw him but Leo as he would be now. He would be forty-eight. She prepared a vista of golden amaranth and saw him striding toward her through the grain. She smelt the fertile soil. Then, she let the image disperse. She held on only to the sense of him—an abstraction containing every single thing about him she remembered. Then, an abstraction with just the whole and none of the particulars. She discarded each detail until she was left with an essence. She willed this sense to be present to her. Right here, in this room.

Chris had taken some time off from her practice for Penelope's visit. Her clients would have to shift for themselves. She knew Nikki, her most difficult case, was as fond of her plump "white-assed face" as she was fond of him. But even he would be fine with the cover she'd arranged.

Fortunately, the weather had broken overnight. The morning was dry and cool. As the day passed, Chris and Penelope found some of the flavor of their camp days coming back to them. Penelope was circumspect but generous, recommending books Chris was truly eager to read.

It was on the second day of the visit, on Tuesday, that Chris brought up the party on Friday. It would be Porchfest in Somerville, when musicians played for passersby from their porches. Penelope briefly closed her eyes. Talia would be back and the four of them would wander the neighborhood. After that, a group of Matt's friends would come by for an after-party of ribs and beer. Some of the wives would come too. Chris let Penelope know there might be a couple of men she wanted her to meet.

"Chris," Penelope sighed, irritated.

"I know. I know. But, I'm not sure either of them will even come. The whole evening is very casual." The two were seated on a blanket by The Charles. Penelope turned to her inner checklist: open, cultivate gratitude, focus on others. She drew in a breath. Reaching within, Penelope was determined not to fall victim to the errors that doomed attraction fundamentals.

"I'm grateful you thought of me in this way . . ."

"But . . ." Chris said. Penelope watched a dog, off-leash, as it sniffed around a bench close to the river and lifted its leg.

"Someone should have that dog on a leash."

"But," repeated Chris. "I felt a 'but' at the end of your sentence." Penelope did not respond immediately.

"It's just: how could you know what I might want?"

"Well, obviously, I don't. As far as I know, you've been by yourself for the last twenty years and that is what you want."

"As far as you know."

"Haven't you been," asked Chris, "alone?"

Penelope didn't answer. She seemed to be absorbed by the untethered dog. Chris tracked a phalanx of college students on break as they wandered by—their young legs in the summer light a Muybridge freeze-frame of perfection.

"You don't need me to tell you, you are still very interesting," continued Chris, "if ethereal."

"Ethereal?"

"You know. Like you don't really live in your body."

"Ah," said Penelope.

"Don't get me wrong. Your things are beautiful. Your body is beautiful inside them, I'm sure. But they're so austere, so butch. Monk-like. You could be a nun."

"Nun or monk or queer?" Penelope laughed. "What are you cooking up Chris, in that sunny head of yours? Are you planning to serve up your match-making with a make-over on the side?"

Chris shook her head.

"I'm talking attitude. Look, you took such good care of me when I was a scared six-year-old. And fat."

"You were never fat."

"I was. I want to return the favor and, since I'm not six now, I can't help wondering what your game-plan is if you don't mean to remain alone but don't plan to inhabit yourself?"

"Incisive, Chris Townsend."

"That's why I get paid the big bucks," said Chris. She lay back on the blanket and closed her eyes. "So?"

"I'm working on it in my own way," said Penelope.

"But you'll meet these guys?" There was a long pause. When Chris was on the brink of giving up, Penelope spoke.

"Yes. I'll meet them."

In the car ride home, after trading notes on their lip-gloss, Talia and Rachel were comparing the tans they'd acquired in just five days on The Cape. Rachel was turning her arm next to Talia's.

"You had a head start," said Rachel.

"Because I'm Italian?"

"Half-Italian," said Rachel.

"Well, I look a lot like my dad."

Rachel turned toward her friend.

"You have some of your mom's features."

"Like what?"

"Her eyes."

"Mine are brown."

"Her eyes, in brown."

Talia exhibited almost no interest in the person, Penelope Wendall, who was in the house on her return—some kind of relative. She was not impressed to learn they had met before, many times, when Talia was little. Talia's attention was on Porchfest. It had already started.

Penelope presented Talia with the newest book by a very popular young adult author. It was an advanced copy. It was signed. Not completely without manners, Talia thanked her. Half an hour later, as they left for the festival, Penelope spied the book, facedown, on a dusty shelf by the door, among the sneakers.

Wandering the sidewalks and pausing to listen every block or so, Penelope found the music jarring. It was a mish mash of styles. It was uneven. She oriented toward the community feeling to ground herself. Only her commitment to manifestation made the adventure tolerable. Openness, she reminded herself. Chris and Talia, with a list in hand, steered the three of them from porch to porch. Matt had stayed behind to smoke the ribs. He might join them, in a bit, at a designated stoop, where a trio he liked played a mean banjo. Penelope believed the selection process, largely Talia's, was driven by which neighborhood bands had the cutest guys. Chris indulged her daughter, giving in to her over and over. Knowing nothing of bringing up kids, Penelope imagined this was likely to end badly.

Eventually, Penelope, Chris, and Talia reached the porch where they were supposed to rendezvous with Matt. Sure enough, there he was, surrounded by a group of other dads, beer in hand, a grin across his face. His head was bopping in rhythm but stopped when the lead banjo moved into a solo with major picking licks. This display wrapped up the song at a rousing tempo. Matt's whoop was louder than the others. Penelope noticed Talia looked swept up too. For this brief number, her eyes shone with a different focus. Penelope couldn't tell what it was.

"Wasn't that great?" said Matt turning to Penelope and clapping loudly. Penelope nodded, doing her best to appear enthusiastic. This would be the last stop before they turned back for the party. Dread darkened the cheerful scene. Fear is constriction, she thought.

"Did you know Talia plays?" asked Matt.

"I did not."

"That's her teacher." Chris pointed.

"The tall one on the left?"

"No. The one in the striped shirt with the unbuttoned cuffs."

"Ah," said Penelope, "the soloist." Twenty or so, he was the most handsome.

The band had started up again, making speech difficult, but both parents nodded confirmation. Talia had moved as close as possible to the band. From where Penelope stood, she could see Talia's eyes on this young man's fingers as they plucked the strings. With a start, Penelope realized that Talia's eyes were like her own: close to the surface of her face. They were busy absorbing the moves.

By six, Matt and a buddy had a folding table on its back. They joked while they clicked its legs into place. Paper goods were stacked here and there in unsteady towers. Chris and another woman were unlocking the French doors from the bottom. These they swung wide and secured to the outer wall of the house. Penelope marveled at how much had been left to the last minute, how much activity was underway, yet how unstressed her hosts seemed. Recorded music was already playing in the background. The smell of barbequed ribs filled the room.

She would master her reflex to run away. Having witnessed a version of her own eyes in Talia's, she remembered it was possible to drink in the world without cowardice. But first she would allow herself to regroup upstairs.

Opening the door to her terrace, she could barely believe how deeply she needed the sanctuary of her room. She turned on the floor fan and lay spread across her coverlet. After ten minutes, she got up and showered. She opened her bag. She lifted out a pair of wide white linen pants and a white scoop-necked shell. She dug for her strand of chalcedony beads. They were translucent, white with a sapphire blue cast. The necklace had a single golden tassel. On the back of the closet door, she found a full-length mirror. Monk-like, she thought. Definitely. She went back into the bathroom and fished around. In a drawer of the rickety vanity were some bobby pins. She clipped her hair up off her neck. She went to the extraordinary length of trying a frank red lipstick she discovered rolling around the drawer, even though it was used. She returned to the mirror. Now, no one could call this look austere. The simplicity of her clothes offset her mouth. Her red lips made her eyes look very much like the beads she was wearing, only bluer. Her sandals had been left by the front door, so she headed downstairs barefoot.

Almost immediately, Chris approached her and steered her toward the balcony. Looking her over, Chris said, "Brava. Come with me. I have someone I want you to meet."

Penelope was to be thrown in at the deep end. She clung to the image of swimming. Air would keep her afloat. Sealing her lips she expanded her lungs through her nose for buoyancy and to increase the flow of *prana*. They pushed through the accumulating crowd to the outside. Penelope instantly spotted the target. A tall man, Matt's age, was speaking with a couple. He had an impressive jaw and a bedhead of salt and pepper hair.

Even from a distance, she noticed the way he listened to the pair, his long body making a graceful arc. Penelope's strict policy of keeping expectations low was paying off. This was not the first attempt that had been made on her behalf. Appraising the attractive stranger, she thought, it will not be the last.

"Troy, hi," began Chris touching his arm without bothering to wait for a break in the conversation. "This is my cousin Penelope."

Troy turned away from the couple toward the two women.

"Hi, Penelope."

"Hi."

"Troy is a journalist. He travels all the time," said Chris. "And Penelope is a book worm. She never travels anywhere." Chris looked back and forth between them as if this were the prefect reason for them to meet. Taking in their hesitation, she added, "Discuss." Penelope and Troy, both denizens of college towns, laughed at the prompt. Chris, seeing her work was done, called over her shoulder, "Matt, don't put those out yet." She turned back to face Penelope and Troy only long enough to say, "Excuse me," before heading off to correct Matt's timing.

"Well, well. 'Troy' and 'Penelope', what are the chances?" said Penelope.

"Slim," said Troy, "can I get you a drink?" Here was the first challenge. The half glass of wine had been more than enough for her that first night. She didn't drink. But in the spirit of openness, Penelope agreed to the evening's cocktail. Nothing ventured. As he went on this mission, she looked at the couple who had been so easily dropped. They lifted their chins and turned back inside. For a moment, she was alone. Penelope glanced back after them. She could see that, despite Chris's bid for delay, the food was out and people were beginning to fill their plates. Let him not return with a plate for me, she thought. She wasn't hungry. She looked out across the lawns. Through the competing aroma of the cookout, the rose reached her. She felt a pleasant weight in her limbs as she recognized its luxurious sweetness. For an instant, she considered the merits of escaping back upstairs to her room. She fingered the gold tassel on her chest. Then, Troy was back with their drinks.

"Here you go," he said, handing her the glass with its salted rim.

"Thank you," she said as they clinked glasses. "Cheers."

"I didn't get you ribs but I did check the supply. We can safely wait without sacrificing Matt's fantastic ribs."

"Are they very good?"

"They are." Troy took a swig of his drink. "Wow. This is good too. Tasty but strong."

Penelope tried hers. "Whoo," she exhaled, stunned.

"Jalapeno and lime."

"Ah. I'll have to drink this carefully." When Troy didn't respond, she said, "So are you one of the famous grade school chums?"

"I am the only famous one," said Troy. Seeing her forced smile he added, "Yes. Guilty as charged. Born and raised in Arlington."

"Does that account for your Wanderlust?"

He smiled back at her. "Maybe. How 'bout you? What accounts for your . . . for your," he stumbled before settling on, "non-nomadic contentment?"

"Who said I was content?"

"But it's true you don't travel?"

"Yes."

"Why?"

"I prefer to receive the wider world through report."

"I see, now, why Chris wanted us to meet."

"How's that?"

"You like reports. I'm a reporter."

This time, Penelope laughed. She could not help herself from a shift upwards in her assessment of this stranger. Taking another tentative sip, she felt the searing warmth in her gullet. Her anxiety lifted slowly, counterbalanced by a growing languid weight in her arms, as the drink gradually hit its mark. A foreign correspondent, formerly with *The Globe*, Troy had been on the ground when Gaddafi had been deposed. Penelope listened closely, marveling at this bravery. Suddenly, he interrupted himself to ask if she minded if they got their ribs now. He was hungry. Penelope reminded herself it was all part of the project. She sealed her lips again and drew in air, nodding, yes.

They set off together toward the banquet table. The packed room slowed them. Penelope squeezed by the guests a second time, touching hot skin through summer clothes. The spicy Margaritas had combined with the warm evening to loosen the crowd. Before they crossed the room, Chris was again at Penelope's elbow.

Leaning in, Chris yelled, "Troy, may I borrow my cousin for a moment?"

Troy said, "Sure," and bent down to ask Penelope, "Shall I get you a plate?"

"Yes, please. I'll be right back."

"OK. Meet you outside."

Penelope nodded and allowed herself to be peeled away toward the far end of the room. A knot of people were laughing. They formed a half-circle around a delicate dark fellow. As this group ate the messy meal off paper plates, he entertained them. Their stained fingers held ribs and napkins destroyed by use. Women ate as daintily as possible—difficult, Penelope thought, watching them tear the meat from bone with their teeth. She studied the man's rapid delivery.

"The new approach has flipped that dynamic. My students watch my lectures online and come prepared to do the problem sets in the classroom. Easier for me. Easier for them. When I perform in private, it's a better show."

Penelope felt a wave of general approval pass through the group. A woman, Penelope thought a mom, was about to ask a question when Chris took the man's arm.

"Excuse me, Geoffrey, may I steal you for a second," said Chris without wasting time. Geoffrey turned toward her and, seeing Penelope, moved away from his group.

"Hold that thought," said Geoffrey, over his shoulder, to the inquiring mother.

"Geoff, this is my cousin, Penelope."

"Hello," he said. It was obvious to Penelope he'd been told to expect the meeting. Chris had certainly primed the pump. Look at you, young cousin, thought Penelope.

"Hi," said Penelope, holding out her hand.

"Geoff, Penelope owns a very successful book store out near Amherst. Penelope, Geoff teaches math to high school students but was an assistant professor at Amherst years ago."

"Oh," said Penelope, as they shook hands. "Didn't you like it at Amherst?"

"It was more they didn't like me. The damn tenure system." At this, without ceremony, Chris left them.

"Ah, well, that is too bad." Penelope had to speak loudly through the din. She nervously watched Chris' retreating back and, beyond her, Troy making his way back to their spot. Geoff laughed. He was extremely handsome. Particularly when laughing. She had the strong impression he knew this.

"No, no. I don't mean I failed a tenure review. It never came to that. I had a temporary appointment out of grad school but there was no opening on the permanent faculty. This was ages ago— almost twenty years. There were things calling me to the Boston area, matters of the heart, so I shoved off for greener pastures." He waved his hands in an animated way. "I've been ever so happily running the math department at BB & N for years."

"Buckingham, Browne and Nichols. Math," said Penelope.

"Yes." He paused and looked at Penelope brightly. "I wish we called it maths like the Brits."

"Really? Because it is so many different things?"

"No. I just like the way it sounds." He looked about. "Listen, you don't seem to have a plate."

"I do. Someone called Troy is getting me one." An eyebrow shot up above Geoff's beautiful eyes.

"Troy? Damn his socks. Such an adventurer."

"Are you warning me away?" Penelope laughed. Lowering his voice, Geoff leaned closer.

"Not unless you want me to."

He was flirting. In return, she reached out and, to her own amazement, touched his sleeve. "I better go find him but are you staying? I can circle back in a bit." Geoff looked at her intensely with a query on his face. Penelope tried to leave her face blank. He moved in to speak in her ear.

"If you're staying, I'm staying." His breath on her ear sent an electric shock through her. She stood up straight.

"OK, then. See you in a few," Penelope shouted over the noise.

.   .   .

When Penelope returned, Troy was speaking with a young woman with a long braid. This person had her face tipped up to speak with him. Troy was holding two plates. Because of his height, the woman's braid hung away from her back. Penelope observed her freckled shoulders and the youthful curve of her spine.

"That's fascinating," she was saying as Penelope approached. A possessive contraction made Penelope narrow her eyes. Troy caught this look and threw back his head in an unrestrained laugh. The young woman looked startled and glanced behind her at Penelope.

The woman looked back and forth between them. "Oh. I didn't know."

Troy shook his head as if in silent apology for having created the confusion while handing Penelope her plate.

"Here you are, dear," he said, like an old married man. "This is Bea. Beatrice. She teaches yoga to Chris. Bea, this is Chris's cousin, Penelope, also a yogi."

"Hello," said Penelope, "nice to meet you." The young woman widened her wide-set eyes.

"Hi," said Bea, "I better get myself some of those before they're gone." She pushed her way back into the living room. Penelope looked her censure at Troy.

"Now, now," said Troy, maintaining the spousal tone.

"That was pretty high school of you."

"There is a big grade school presence here. I think the source of bad behavior is earlier."

"How did you know I do yoga?"

"A guess."

"Please don't let me interfere if you want . . ."

"No, thanks. Not interested." He followed the other woman's form with his eyes. "I think she's twelve."

Penelope looked over her shoulder. "Thirty at least."

"Same difference."

"OK. Whatever. Thanks for these," said Penelope accepting the plate. "I met another of your old classmates, Geoffrey somebody. He teaches math. He wishes it were called maths."

"Oh, no, Geoff," said Troy. Now, it was his turn to narrow his eyes.

"What is it with you two? I thought Matt kept a whole 'kumbaya' thing going among you guys."

"We have been competing since second grade."

"What? All of you?"

"No, just Geoff and me."

"Why?"

"I was king of the hill when Geoff arrived from Hawaii."

"He stole your thunder at six?"

"Seven. Yes. He was ridiculously good at everything, not just numbers. Plus unbearably cute. All the girls, and most of the teachers, were gaga over him."

"Sounds awful," said Penelope.

"We had high hopes he'd left the field when he settled down at twenty-five but the marriage didn't last."

"A pity."

"She tired of his obsession."

"She tired of math?"

"Not that."

"Oh?"

"She tired of Geoffrey."

"I see." Penelope thought over Geoff's manner. "Still, you have to admit he has charisma."

"Oh, I know," said Troy in a friendlier tone. "He does. I wouldn't mind but he is always snapping up the best women."

Penelope shook her head in disbelief and took a bite of her ribs.

"That sounds Neanderthal. Speaking of which, these are good."

"Told you."

She looked at him amused. "Was that thing with the girl some ape-y move to 'snap me up'?"

Troy smiled broadly and aimed his jaw toward her. "You are nothing like your cousin's description."

"So she did do some spade work."

"Yeah, some. Not much. But I did expect a dishy new-age librarian."

"Sorry to disappoint."

Troy raised his eyes to hers. He waited. Penelope finished her drink in one long pull. Troy put his gnawed bone back on the plate and wiped his lips. "It's the librarian part. Is it rude of me to point out how beautiful you are?" Penelope blushed like a kid. "Hey, do you want to get out of here?" He was leaning down toward her as he said this. He has watched danger unfold around him, Penelope thought. He likes that, to be close to danger. In that moment, she was aware how much this reminded her of Leo. He continued to look at her, to probe her with his eyes. She dropped her head, embarrassed.

"Wow. You're direct."

"Yeah, war zone stuff. I'm sorry if I'm misreading signals."

Penelope looked up at him. "Chris mentioned I'm a recluse."

"So?"

"Maybe we could do a less exciting thing first, like go some-place we can actually speak?"

"How long are you staying?"

"I'm here 'till Tuesday morning."

"Dinner then?"

"Yes."

"I'll call."

"OK."

Juggling their food, they traded contacts with their phones. Penelope watched his forearms as he swiped, searched and sent his. After the necessary banter to accomplish this, a silence dropped over them but they did not move apart. They finished their food. Penelope felt foolish. Whatever is my problem, she thought.

"Here let me take that," he said as he reached for her empty plate. Gathering both plates in one hand, he took the napkin in his other and wet a corner with his tongue. With the damp edge proffered he asked, "May I?" Without waiting for her assent, he wiped away a spot of barbeque sauce from her cheek. The gesture was less like a player than a pal. "I'll be in touch," he said in a lowered voice.

"Thanks. Yes. OK," said Penelope.

Troy turned away. Penelope stood her ground. She felt definitely light-headed. She watched him pass through the living room. She saw him exchange a few words with Geoff. What were they saying? Geoff's face widened in a grin and he looked toward her as Troy moved away. Seeing Geoff's game face, Penelope felt a stab of unanchored longing. She turned her head without acknowledging him. Again, the Secret Rose's honey reached her. She drank in a long breath and closed her eyes. Her body swayed slightly. She didn't care. It did not matter if other guests noticed her. She took a full minute to come back to herself and to visualize Leo in the grain.

When she opened her eyes, Geoff was beside her.

"Meditating?"

"Sort of."

"I've brought you another drink," he said holding out a fresh glass. She reached for it as if from a trance. He watched her take a mouthful.

"Thirsty?"

Penelope nodded.

"Your friend, Troy, seems to have made an impression," said Geoff.

"Why do you say my friend? You are the two who have known each other for eons."

"Forty-one years, to be exact."

"And the playground rivalry continues?" Penelope sipped again. The salty top tasted wonderful as the heat spread through her chest.

"Is that what he said?"

"Mm Hmm."

"Well, I think he was having you on. We love each other."

Penelope's eyebrows shot up.

"Don't look so skeptical. He took to you and was playing fast."

"But you were the one who said he is an adventurer."

"I did, didn't I. Well, let's not fritter away another moment on him. I do adore Troy but I'm so much more interested in you. Tell me, for instance, about your meditation practice. Or your bookstore."

Penelope felt the tidal wave of charm from before as she bent her head over the rim of the drink. Oh, Chris, what have you done? Penelope attempted to root herself to the shifting ground.

"Tell me first about yourself. Troy said you were married?" To her surprise, Geoff's mouth tightened in pain.

"She was the love of my life," said Geoff, straight.

"Oh. I'm sorry. I shouldn't have brought it up."

"It's all right. How could you know?"

Penelope shook her head as if she should have. She took another sip. Then, a long swallow. Caution, she realized dimly, had left her.

"Did she fall for someone else?"

"No. It was me."

"But, Troy said she left you?"

Geoff cut his eyes at her, his sparkle returning.

"He did move quickly," he said approvingly. Then he paused as if sizing her up. "It wasn't an affair. I was smitten with a student. That was all. Wildly inappropriate in so many ways. I was married. He was my student. He was only eighteen.

Penelope took this in.

"I see. You told your wife?"

"Yes. She was shocked."

"That you are bisexual?"

"No, no. She knew that going into the marriage. Anyway, whatever that pan-appetite was, it has faded with age. Things seem to simplify. Have you found that?" He did not wait for Penelope to answer. "In any case, what bothered her was the boy's age. I explained to her it was just a crush. The body has its wants. One can control one's behavior but not one's desires. Don't you think?"

"I suppose."

"You suppose?" laughed Geoff, brightening. "Really, this is something one knows or doesn't. It is a matter of direct experience."

The force of her persistent longing for Leo swept over her. Her eyes filled with tears. "What have I done," cried Geoff, seeing her distress.

"Nothing," said Penelope, drying her eyes. Geoff watched her. There was a quick gentleness in his expression.

"Is it the fiancé?" he hazarded.

"Jesus, what did Chris tell you?"

"Very little," he said, echoing Troy, "just that there was someone and he was lost."

"Yes. Lost."

"I am so sorry."

Penelope shook her head. Her beads slid back and forth across her chest. Tenderly, Geoff took the tassel and held it as if steadying her.

"We share this, then," he said, "lost loves." She nodded. He released her necklace. "Great loves," he whispered. Troy was wrong about him, thought Penelope.

"Wow," said Penelope. "I'm dizzy with the speed I'm falling for every person in sight." Geoff twinkled.

"I think it's the tequila," he said.

"Ah. Right you are," said Penelope. She drained the rest of her drink as if it were a shot and smiled at Geoff with her whole face. Maybe this was the vehicle she needed. Then, the ground tipped abruptly. "I need to lie down," she said, reconsidering. She heard how muddled her voice sounded, as if from outside.

"May I help you?"

"That would be very kind of you. I'm upstairs."

When Geoff opened the door to her room, Penelope turned toward him.

"Are you going to ask me in?" he asked eagerly.

"No. Not while I'm drunk."

"Damn."

"But I'm here for another three days. Shall we see each other again?"

"Oh, absolutely. This has been the funniest introduction. But, I'm truly delighted to have met you." Geoff tipped his head to the side and regarded her with the quick interest of a bird.

"I must be mad," said Penelope. "I offered Troy too," she slurred.

"The blackguard," said Geoff. "No matter, I will best him." At this, Penelope threw her arms around Geoff and planted a full kiss on his mouth. When she pulled back he gave her a satisfied look, brought the golden tassel to his mouth, and kissed it.

"I'll call Matt for your contact."

"No, Chris, please."

"I'll call Chris, then. Until soon."

"Soon," said Penelope as she shut the door.

She stumbled to the upholstered stool and dropped her linen pants and top there. She slipped out of her bra but left on her panties and the beads. She slid under the bedclothes, closing her eyes. Her mind was throbbing. She thought of Talia with her eyes on the cords. The voraciousness of youth and its velocity flitted through her. She thought of herself now, a bookseller, and how a story is built of narrative strands shot back and forth through events. She thought of the two men. Why were they both so keen? Had she manifested them? She plucked at the selvage of the coverlet, a loosely woven thing. Was her intention knitting itself together or unraveling? She tried to remember the two reasons most manifestation projects fail. One: a blockage of the heart. What was the other? Even though she was lying down she tried to conjure Leo. But he would not come to her. Instead, she saw an ocean. The rocking of its waves gave her the spins. She opened her eyes. She needed air.

Penelope sat up and slipped back out of bed. She walked over to the French doors. She opened them and stepped out. The tequila was humming through her. She could hear happy voices below. Being almost naked above the party aroused her. When last had anything felt this good? Stretching her arms, she took a deep breath. She closed her eyes, again. The swimming was instantaneous. She danced a few steps then staggered a few and giggled. I am twenty-six, she thought. She breathed in, wobbling, and called Leo to her. What swept over her instead had some of the pressure of Troy and some of the quickness of Geoff. The ocean returned. On it a vast wooden boat was bearing down. She swayed in response and felt the rough peeling paint of the balustrade graze her thigh. At just this moment, there was a sharp knocking at the door. Reeling, she tried to catch herself with her open palms against the rail. There was another knock—a single one, but loud.

"Are you all right?" a voice asked through the door.

"Yes," said Penelope, not recognizing her own voice as her palms met the railing.

"I've brought something for you," he said. Where had she heard this person before? The door made it difficult to make him out.

"Slip it under. I'm not dressed," she called without opening her eyes.

There was no answer. In the silence, Penelope realized whatever this was, whoever this was, had come in answer. She pictured a shadow falling across the lintel. A stem shook, as it appeared, with thorns, pushed by an unsteady hand. Penelope pictured her hands on the smooth wood of the door. She opened them outward as if caressing its promise. The sharp flakes of paint on the rail cut her hands.

"Ah," she cried. Still, she did not open her eyes. Penelope imagined looking down at the light seeping under the door to see more leaves and more thorns, appearing. She lifted one hand into space as if to grasp the imaginary stem.

"Oh," she said out loud, "I'm pricked." Without realizing it, she was cantilevered over the balustrade, three stories above the garden. On the screen of her closed eyelids, she saw the flower head caught on the bottom of the door. She could hear the German accent when he spoke again. She turned toward it. She thought he called, *pull*. Penelope reached away from the railing back toward the door to give a stronger tug so the compressed flower could slide under.

As soon as it was through, it opened with her eyes.

Test Subjects

. . . And the sweepstakes winner, the three-some, the gymnast, the short seller, the pop star, the larper, the linguist, the gerrymanderer, the horndog, the saint, the teller, the trans, the toddler, the bitch slapper, the bro, the cute checkout guy, the lefty, the loonie, the shakers and the fakirs and the fakers shall lie down together like the lion and the lamb. They will just lie the fuck down because there is no insurance policy with enough contingencies, no long game long enough. That's what Sarah thinks as she digs the hole for Zander's guinea pig, Elijah. That and how worthless is every scrap of her ambition. The world is full of people with crazy talents. Full even of people with a special set of pipes.

Sarah finishes burying Elijah. She doesn't have a hold on the natural lifespan of guinea pigs. Elijah did not seem old. She tries to remember when his sweet fusty body came into their lives. It must have been when the bomb of their mom, Julia's, cancer went off. Sarah wonders if, when guinea pigs expire, they release a bolus of light from their crowns like the sadhus in the Hindu comic book—a book Julia gave Zander when he was five. That was only three years ago. This means Elijah probably came to them having already done a few laps around some other cage.

Thinking of cages, Sarah pictures Elijah's cowlick-y fur, how it swirled in every direction, and then her mom's dying face, still pretty when she exhaled. With her eyes closed, her last breath had blown out of her like an expression of wonder, as if doors had sprung wide on a surprise party thrown by friends.

This makes Sarah think of her mom's friends. She remembers it was Yvette, Julia's brilliant funny friend, the famous writer and animal lover, who gave Elijah to them. Yvette keeps a zoo's-worth of pets, including Angoras for Mohair. Once Julia sent her a link to a pair of sandals with fur-lined foot-beds when her friend was feeling broke and low. Yvette said she might just collect the ambient dog hair and tape it to her feet to achieve the same effect at a deep discount. Sarah thinks, hallelujah for this adult who once gave Zander a blowtorch to finish some crème brûlée she was serving. A miracle he hadn't swung around and ignited Yvette. Who gives an eight-year-old a blowtorch? Sarah guesses the same kind of person who gave him a creature to care for when his world was coming apart.

The reflection cheers Sarah a little although it doesn't erase her dread of compounding Zander's gravity with Elijah's death. Whose plan was it for her to be in charge of such things at eighteen? In charge of the way Zander's eyes are too wide. Sarah sighs. There is no plan.

But when Zander comes home, he takes it in stride. He's lost bigger things. He just asks for the details and nods. When Sarah tells him she took care of the burial, he nods again.

"But we should throw him a party," Zander says.

So on Friday, Sarah decorates the living room with pictures of Elijah she had enlarged at Staples and a few of Julia's paintings of shrews. Sarah puts out bowls of carrots and shredded lettuce, Elijah's favorite foods. Once in a while she suspects the husbands didn't stick because her mom worked directly from life—all those rodents around, particularly the shrews. But she doubts that's it really. Why they left.

When husband two disappeared into thin air, Julia, the least practical of people, had the impulse to buy a life insurance policy. Sarah wonders sometimes if Julia had a premonition. In any event, the timing was lucky. Zander's dad's departure, the purchase, and the discovery of Julia's malignancy followed each other lickety-split. The policy didn't keep Julia from pain but it kept Sarah and Zander now. It is good for party funds. Good for a lot of things.

Sarah invites a dozen people for 3 p.m., half an hour before Zander gets home from school. She asks his three best buds, their moms, Yvette and four of Julia's other closest friends. Even though it's a wake and not a birthday party, Sarah wants Zander to find a celebration when he gets home.

When Yvette comes over to help, she smiles approvingly at the decorations but says, "Is that what you're giving people to eat?" Sarah looks again at the guinea pig food and wishes there were something else. Yvette shakes her head cheerfully. "Don't worry. Pre-heat the oven to 400. I'll be back in a flash."

By the time the guests arrive, crostini have been added to the carrot and salad offerings. Wine and juice glasses are at the ready on the dining room table. Next to these, Sarah splays small square napkins with owls on them. She wonders if there are owls in the Andes where Elijah's kind are native. If so, they are probably guinea pigs' predators. She hopes this doesn't cross Zander's mind. Animal and napkin-wise, it was the best she could do.

Two of the early arrivals, Frederico, a designer, and Joe, his partner, come at Sarah with questions about where she is with her playlist of new songs. Sarah doesn't tell them she has recorded three recently. Federico swipes across his phone searching for a picture. Like all of Julia's friends, Frederico worships

Sarah. He shows her the image. It's a mock-up of an album cover he designed for whenever she is brave enough to put out her first EP. The cover is a pastiche of guinea pig faces in sixties pop styling. Their cheeks and tear-drop eyes loan themselves to this treatment. The mock-up title he used is her band's name, *Test Subjects*.

"It's perfect," gasps Sarah, kissing him. Over near the white couch (the one unstained item in Sarah and Zander's apartment) Yvette and Sonny are in boisterous conversation, their juice glasses filled with red wine. Sarah spies Sonny, who broke his foot a week ago, using his crutches to rock back on his heels while Yvette laughs at a story he is telling.

"Hold up," shouts Sarah, "watch-out for the couch." But the warning causes the accident Sarah was hoping to avoid. As Yvette turns toward Sarah's cry, her bell sleeve catches on Sonny's crutch. It is a glancing catch but enough to tip her hand. A gloosh of wine escapes and splatters across the cushions.

Yvette instructs Sarah to salt the couch and lift the stain with soda water. While Sarah is madly pursuing this, Zander comes in. She's so immersed in the cleanup, Yvette has to alert her by touching her shoulder. Sarah's efforts, so far, have turned the fabric a watery rose. Sarah waves the large soda bottle at her brother before relinquishing it to Yvette. Zander smiles back through the group and the decorations. He is hugging a square of day glow pink paper to his chest. It is the same pink as kumkum powder, a powder Hindus use to douse themselves during rituals or dot their foreheads where they believe the third eye can open.

Zander makes straight for Sarah. He is impeded by well-wishers until they realize he's on a mission. They let him pass. She can see, when he gets to her, he is trembling.

"What do you have there?" she asks. Zander doesn't answer. Instead he turns the sheet toward her. It's an abstraction. The pink of the paper below shows the whorls of textured design radiating outward. The effect is stunning. A masterpiece in macaroni.

"What is it?"

"It's a picture of Elijah," says Zander, who is himself radiant.

"What is he doing?" asks Sarah, squinting at the page. Zander looks at Sarah curiously as if she should be able to tell.

"It's his Mahasamadhi."

"I don't know what that is, Zander."

"Elijah has arrived," Zander says.

Sarah wraps an arm around Zander's head and knuckle-rubs his hair. "Let's set him a place," she says.

Acknowledgements

I would like to thank David Blumel, of Tall Island Press, Grace Ross and Carolyn Jourdan for their advice on preparing this book to move it out into the world. To the friends and writers who have been called on, over the last four years, in an unusual way, I also owe an enormous debt. Fate put me in need of community not only to support my writing but to support me through the hiatus from writing that stretched over an agonized three of those years. Those who rallied round are too numerous to mention by name—the many who turned up with open arms, as counsel, comfort, spiritual guides, and writing inspiration. I am infinitely grateful to all of you. Among this crowd were the giants that held up my firmament: Jessica Helfand, Sharon Garbe, Bobby Houston, Eric Shamie, Gundula Brattke, Maria Nation, Roberto Flores, Robin and Dai Ban, Bob Massie, Anne Tate, Mary Pat Akers, Julia Kidd, David Cabrera, Amy Lipton, Julie Scott, Jim Hall, Hester Velmens, Anne McDonald, Dabney MacAvoy, Jeff Nunokawa, Susan Merchant, Jamie Akers, Mariana Cicerchia, Betsy Spears, Barbara Friedman, Bob Dow, Billie Best, Karen Cole and Michael Kink. Thank you from the bottom of my heart. I simply would not have survived to write these stories without my tireless sage of a spouse, Michael Lipson, my insanely brave son, Rody, and the essential Abigail Lipson, Jennie Wright, Gardiner Morse, Sarah Lee and Craig-O Nicholson.

This collection was written between October 2015 and October 2016, as I took steps back toward life from the realms of illness and grief. The stories collected here represent part of my effort to meet the challenge our eldest son explicitly left: to find in his death a source of positivity. So, both first and last, I want to thank Asher Lipson, to whom this book is dedicated, who brought me, along with the gifts of his brilliance, wit, and sweetness, a glittered souvenir Colosseum that changed color— not with the local weather as advertised, but, Asher thought, perhaps with the weather in Rome or my inner weather.

About the Author

Holly Morse is an artist and writer. With her husband Michael Lipson, PhD, she is writing *I Say Hello,* an epistolary collaboration that explores love, loss and the nature of time. Morse is a graduate of The California Institute of the Arts MFA program. She lives with her family in the Berkshires of Western Massachusetts.

CPSIA information can be obtained
at www.ICGtesting.com
Printed in the USA
FFOW03n1948090617
36482FF